A faint smile curved his lips.

"I'm a curious man and you're a beautiful woman. A plus B equals C."

"That's not the way algebra works."

Finn chuckled lowly. "You're right. That's not algebra. That's my own special equation."

He was making light of the whole thing and it would be best if she did, too. But his kiss had shaken her to the very depths of her being. And she was sick of men never taking her seriously, tired of being considered a pleasant pastime and nothing more.

"Very cute," she muttered, then quickly turned away from him and walked over to Harry's playpen. "But I've had enough laughs for one night. I'm putting Harry and myself to bed."

Mariah was bending over to pick up Harry when Finn's hands caught her around the waist and tugged her straight back into his arms.

"If you thought that was for laughs, then maybe I'd better do it over."

Before she could react he'd already fastened his lips over hers. And this time there was no mistaking the raw hunger in his kiss.

* * *

MEN OF THE WEST: Whether ranchers or lawmen, these heartbreakers can ride, shoot— and drive a woman crazy...

Dear Reader,

Spring has arrived on the Silver Horn Ranch, and normally at this time of year, the only thing on Finn Calhoun's mind is the babies being born to the ranch's prestigious mares. But Finn's job as manager of the horse division is suddenly interrupted in a big way when he learns that another baby has been born. Only this one doesn't have a mane and tail. He has dimples that closely resemble Finn's and auburn hair to match!

When Finn travels to Stallion Canyon horse ranch in Northern California, his only focus is determining whether the four-month-old baby actually belongs in the Calhoun family. The notion of becoming a father doesn't frighten Finn, but the feelings he gets whenever he's near the boy's aunt are another matter.

Always loyal to his family, Finn has devoted his all to the Silver Horn. But love has a way of changing a man's vision for the future. And suddenly Finn is wondering if it's finally time to follow his dreams.

When I first met the Calhoun clan of brothers, I thought of Finn as the sweetheart of the bunch. I mean, what woman can resist a cowboy that touches a horse with the same tenderness he touches a woman? I hope you'll join me on another trip to the rugged West to see how Finn finally finds the love of his life and the home he's always wanted.

God Bless each trail you ride,

Daddy Wore Spurs

Stella Bagwell

HARLEQUIN® SPECIAL EDITION®

Recycling programs
for this product may
not exist in your area.

ISBN-13: 978-0-373-65899-2

Daddy Wore Spurs

Printed in U.S.A.

www.Harlequin.com

After writing more than eighty books for Harlequin, **Stella Bagwell** still finds it exciting to create new stories and bring her characters to life. She loves all things Western and has been married to her own real cowboy for forty-four years. Living on the south Texas coast, she also enjoys being outdoors and helping her husband care for the horses, cats and dog that call their small ranch home. The couple has one son, who teaches high school mathematics and is also an athletic director. Stella loves hearing from readers. They can contact her at stellabagwell@gmail.com.

Books by Stella Bagwell

Harlequin Special Edition

Men of the West

The Lawman's Noelle
Wearing the Rancher's Ring
One Tall, Dusty Cowboy
A Daddy for Dillon
The Baby Truth
The Doctor's Calling
His Texas Baby
Christmas with the Mustang Man
His Medicine Woman
Daddy's Double Duty
His Texas Wildflower
The Deputy's Lost and Found
Branded with his Baby
Lone Star Daddy

Montana Mavericks: Striking It Rich

Paging Dr. Right

The Fortunes of Texas

The Heiress and the Sheriff

Visit the Author Profile page at Harlequin.com for more titles.

To my husband, Harrell.
You still look sexy in spurs, my darlin'!

Chapter One

Was this baby his son?

Finn Calhoun stared in wonder at the four-month-old boy cradled in the woman's arms. The child's hair was curly, but it wasn't bright copper like his own. Still, it was a light shade of auburn. Finn's eyes were the color of the sky, while the baby's eyes were a much darker blue. There were also the dimples creasing his fat little cheeks. Finn possessed those same dimples, too. But that was hardly proof the little guy belonged to him.

A man was supposed to have nine months to adjust to the idea of becoming a dad, Finn thought. He'd had all of two days to ponder the notion of having a child. And though he liked to consider himself a man with his boots firmly planted on the ground, the idea that he might be a father had left him feeling as if he'd been shot out of a cannon and hadn't yet landed.

"Would you like to hold him?"

The gently spoken question broke through Finn's dazed thoughts, and he lifted his gaze to Mariah Montgomery, the baby's aunt.

Gauging her to be in her midtwenties, he noted that her slender frame was concealed beneath a pair of worn blue jeans and a sleeveless red checked blouse. Crow-black hair waved back from a wide forehead and was fastened at the nape of her neck with a white silk scarf. Cool gray eyes regarded him with cautious regard, while a set of pale pink lips pressed into a straight line.

Since meeting him at the door five minutes ago and inviting him into the house, Finn hadn't seen any sort of pleasurable expression or welcoming smile cross her face. But Finn could overlook her somber attitude. She'd surely gone through hell these past few weeks.

A month ago, her sister Aimee had died in a skiing accident. Since then she'd had to deal with grief and instant motherhood. Now she was meeting Finn for the first time. And she had no idea if he was a worthless bum who'd taken advantage of her late sister, or a nice guy who'd been caught up in a long-distance love affair. She only knew that Finn's name was listed on the baby's birth certificate as the father.

His head whirling with questions and reservations, Finn stepped forward. "Do you think holding him would be all right?"

She shot him an odd, almost suspicious look. "Why wouldn't it be all right? Fathers do hold their sons. And Aimee named you as the father."

Her voice held a thread of skepticism. As though she was far from convinced he was the boy's father. Well, Finn could've told her that for the past two days, he'd

also been swamped with doubts. No matter that the tim-
ing of the child's birth calculated perfectly back to the
weekend he'd spent with Aimee, a two-day affair hadn't
necessarily created a baby. Even so, he wasn't about to
dismiss the possibility that he was the father.

Keeping these thoughts to himself, he said, "Some
babies don't appreciate being handed over to a stranger.
And I don't want to make him cry."

Mild surprise pushed the suspicion from her face.
"Oh. So you're familiar with babies?"

"I've never had one of my own," he admitted. "But
I spent quite a bit of time with my nieces and nephews
when they were small."

That hardly seemed to impress her, but she did move
a step closer.

"I see. Well, Harry is a friendly little guy. He likes most
everyone."

The breath suddenly rushed from Finn's lungs. "Harry?
Is that short for Harrison?" he asked, his voice little more
than a hoarse whisper.

"That's right. I always call him Harry, though."

The yellow and blue furnishings of the nursery faded
to a dazed blur, prompting Finn to wipe a hand over his
face. He'd never felt so humbled, so shaken in his life.

"Harrison is my first name," he told her. "But I—I
guess you already knew that. You saw it on the birth
certificate."

Her cool gray gaze connected with his and for one
brief moment, Finn thought he spotted a flash of com-
passion in her eyes. Could she possibly understand that
his emotions were riding a violent wave? Maybe she understood he wasn't the sort of man who could casually
make a baby, then walk away without a backward glance.

She said, "I'm sorry. When I spoke to you on the telephone, I was so focused on how to give you the news about Aimee that I didn't think to tell you Harry's name."

Hearing that Aimee had died from a tragic accident had been enough to knock Finn sideways. Then before he could recover, she'd hit him with the news of the baby and that supposedly he was the father. After that he'd been too stunned to ask for details. He'd managed to scribble down the child's location and a phone number, and the rest of the conversation had passed in a blur.

"To be honest I don't recall much of our conversation. I was pretty shaken up. All I could think about was getting up here," Finn admitted, then shook his head. "I can't believe Aimee even remembered my first name. Everyone calls me Finn—that's my middle name."

He held his arms out and Mariah carefully handed the boy to him. Once he had the baby's weight cradled safely in the crook of his arm, the realization that he could be touching his son for the very first time swelled his chest with overwhelming emotions.

Bending his head, Finn placed a kiss on the baby's forehead, while unabashed tears burned the back of his eyes. Father or not, he couldn't ignore the deep and sudden connection he felt to the child in his arms.

"This isn't the way a man is supposed to be introduced to his son," he murmured thickly. "The child should be newly born from his mother's womb with his eyes squinched and his skin all red and wrinkled. He should be there to hear him crying and sucking in the first few breaths of his life."

Lifting his head, he looked to Mariah for answers. "If Harry is truly mine, then I've lost so much—memories and moments that I'll never have. Why didn't Aimee tell me she was pregnant?"

With a frustrated shake of her head, she turned and walked to the far side of the nursery. As Finn watched her go, his gaze was instinctively drawn to the sway of her curvy hips encased in faded denim and the long black tail of hair swishing against her back. He hadn't expected Aimee's sister to look so young or pretty. In fact, during the brief time he'd known Aimee, she hadn't said much about her sister. Only that she had one and that the both of them lived on the ranch.

As Finn had made the drive up here to Stallion Canyon in Northern California, he'd held the notion he'd be meeting an older woman with a family of her own, who'd kindly taken in her little nephew until the father could be located. He couldn't have been more wrong. Mariah was an attractive single woman. Not only that, there was a fierce maternal gleam in her eye. One that said she wasn't about to hand Harry over to him without definitive proof.

"Several weeks passed after Harry was born before Aimee finally told me you were the father. After that, I tried to persuade her to contact you, but she always stalled without giving me a reason. I don't know why. Unless it was because some other man actually fathered Harry. Maybe she got tangled up with a married man. Or she didn't want you involved. I'm just as confused as you are about the whole thing."

It was becoming clear to Finn that Aimee hadn't revealed much, if anything, to her sister about their weekend romance in Reno. But he didn't consider that odd. He hadn't said anything about that weekend to his brothers, either. Not until two days ago when he'd learned about the baby. Before then, his time with Aimee had been a private, personal thing.

"I've never been married. I made that clear to Aimee." He shook his head with confusion. "We met and after having a whirlwind weekend together, I thought she'd taken our time together seriously. Before we parted I gave her my number and she promised to keep in touch. But I never heard from her again."

Her expression rueful, she said, "We were sisters, but we had our differences. She didn't talk much to me about her personal life. But after Harry was born—well, we eventually got into a heated argument."

Her wavering voice had broken in spots and as Finn watched her struggle to hold back tears, it suddenly struck him that this whole ordeal was far more difficult for her than it was for him. Mariah had lost a member of her family. Finn's connection to Aimee had been little more than a brief, star-crossed encounter.

Finn was wondering if he should offer some comforting words when she suddenly went on, "I warned her that if something happened to her, Harry would need his father. I didn't— I never thought something actually would happen. I was only trying to push her into contacting you. But then she really died. Now I have to live with those words I said to her. Even though I said them with good intentions."

Finn was suddenly struck with the urge to go to her and place a reassuring arm around her shoulders. But he held back. They'd met only a few minutes ago. She might not appreciate him getting that close. Especially when the two of them appeared to be the only two adults in the house.

"We all say things we wish we could change or take

back," Finn told her. "But in this case I hardly see where you crossed the line. Harry's father should've been contacted long before his birth. I don't understand why she was keeping it a secret."

She made a helpless palms-up gesture. "Frankly, Aimee had been giving me the impression that the father was someone else. A guy she'd been involved with off and on for a long time. When she told me about you and showed me the birth certificate, I was shocked."

Finn's mind was so jammed with questions, he didn't know where to begin or what to think. "What else did she tell you about me?"

Shrugging, she said, "Not much. Just that you lived in Nevada and liked horses. Later, after the accident, I found your number in her address book."

With the baby cuddled safely to his chest, Finn moved across the room to where Mariah was sitting stiffly on the edge of the rocking chair. The two sisters couldn't have been more different, he thought. Where Mariah was dark and petite, Aimee had been tall, with caramel-brown hair and hazel eyes. Their personalities appeared to be equally opposite, too. Aimee had been full of smiles and laughter, whereas this young woman seemed to be all serious business.

"I don't know what to think about all that, Ms. Montgomery. But if she said I'm the father, then I surely must be." He looked down at the precious baby snuggled in the crook of his arm. Three days ago Finn had been a thirty-two-year-old man with nothing on his mind but his job of managing the Silver Horn's horse division. The possibility of having a child never entered his thoughts. Now here he was holding a baby who could very well be his son. The whole thing seemed surreal. "I met Aimee at the mustang training competition in Reno. After the first round was over I made a point of searching her out. To offer a price for her horse. She refused to sell him."

"But she didn't refuse to go to bed with you," Mariah said pointedly.

Her blunt way of putting it spread a wave of heat over his face. More than a year ago, when he'd said goodbye to Aimee, he'd never imagined that anything so life-altering as a baby had occurred between them. And he certainly hadn't expected Aimee to lose her life on a ski slope less than seventy miles from the Silver Horn.

"We spent the weekend together in Reno. It wasn't like either one of us set out to make a baby."

"I'm not so sure about that, Mr. Calhoun."

The suggestive remark caused his jaw to drop. "You think I—"

"Not you," she interrupted. "I'm talking about Aimee. I've always believed she deliberately set out to get pregnant. If not by you—then someone else."

The idea of Aimee using him to get pregnant was incredible. She'd hardly seemed the conniving type. And why would she have done such a thing?

He said, "I'll admit that two days wasn't long enough for me to know everything about Aimee. But I find it hard to believe she was luring me into a pregnancy trap, or shotgun wedding, or anything close to it. She didn't try to attach any strings to me. My mistake was trusting her when she said she was on the pill. But as you can see I'm here and more than ready to take responsibility for Harry."

Bending her head, she said in a low voice, "I'm sorry. I shouldn't have said any of that. When my sister met you in Reno—well, her plans might not have included a baby at all. It's just that she had—"

"Look, if you were going to tell me about Bryce, I already know. She told me how he'd been a longtime boyfriend. But she'd broken things off with him."

Her head popped up. "Aimee mentioned Bryce to you? That's surprising. She wasn't one to share personal things."

"Sometimes it's easier to talk about yourself to someone you just met. Especially if your plans are to never see them again," he added wryly.

Her expression turned curious. "You think she'd never intended to see you again?"

"I didn't then, obviously. But I do now."

The baby began to squirm and Finn looked down to see that the infant was chewing on his tiny fist. Drool was dripping off his chin and Finn carefully wiped it away with his forefinger. Just touching the baby's face and looking into his dark blue eyes filled Finn's heart with a fierce protectiveness. If Harry was his son, he wouldn't let anyone or anything keep him from taking the baby home to the Silver Horn. And that included the black-haired beauty who was eyeing him as though he were the devil himself.

Across the small nursery, Mariah was having all sorts of trouble dragging her gaze away from the rugged Nevada cowboy. A few minutes ago, when she'd opened the door and found herself standing face-to-face with Finn Calhoun, she'd felt as though the ground had shifted beneath her feet.

She'd expected Finn's appearance to be a bit more than average, otherwise Aimee would've never taken a second glance at him. But this guy was leaps and bounds beyond average.

At least two or three inches over six feet, he towered over her. Broad shoulders sat over a long torso that narrowed down to a lean waist and tall, muscular legs. Yet his hard, wiry body was only a part of his striking appearance, she realized. His face was a composite of tough angles and slopes. A jutting chin, hollow cheekbones and rough-hewn lips were softened by a pair of dazzling blue eyes partially hidden by a thick fringe of copper-colored lashes. Slightly darker hair of the same color curled wildly around his ears and against the back of his neck, while a set of white teeth made a startling contrast against his tanned skin.

Oh, he was a looker all right, Mariah decided. But that didn't necessarily make him daddy material. Especially if he used those looks to go around seducing women. Still, in all honesty, she didn't know if this man had done the seducing or if Aimee had been the initiator of their romance. And it hardly mattered now. The only question that should be on her mind was whether he'd actually fathered little Harry.

Reining in her wandering thoughts, Mariah said, "Aimee dated Bryce for over three years and wanted to marry him, but he kept putting her off. He was divorced and wasn't ready to try marriage again. That's why—well, Aimee once told me she was tempted to get pregnant so that Bryce would feel obligated to marry her. But she said he was always too careful about such things and she wasn't sure how she could manage it. I told her she was crazy to even consider such a scheme. Being pregnant wouldn't necessarily force Bryce into marrying her, anyway."

His eyes narrowed with suspicion and Mariah could see that he was stung by the notion that Aimee might have used him, especially to coerce another man into marrying her.

"That's one of the most conniving, deceitful things I've ever heard. If that's the way Aimee's mind worked, then she might've had other affairs. Harry's father might be someone you never heard of!"

The anguished look on his face implied he wanted Harry to be his son. The notion surprised Mariah. Most single guys his age would be running backward at the idea of taking on the responsibility of a baby.

Her gaze continued to roam his rugged face and the big hands gently cradling the baby. "Look, I'm just saying she harbored those ideas. I have no proof she was trying to carry them out with you or any man. For my sister's sake, I'd like to think Harry was innocently conceived."

"With me?"

An awkward silence followed his question, and with each second that passed, the more Mariah had to fight to keep from jumping from the rocker and rushing out of the nursery. Something about this man and her sister sharing a passionate weekend together was an image she wanted to push from her mind.

"Well, I'd hate to think she falsely put your name on the birth certificate. And I'd sure hate to think that Harry's father might always be a question mark."

He looked down at the baby. "I'd never let that happen to this little guy."

Feeling like a jumble of raw nerves, she restlessly crossed her legs and began to tap the air with her bare foot. The movement must have caught his attention because she suddenly noticed his gaze slowly slipping from her face and traveling downward, over her leg and onto her foot.

Heat instantly flooded her cheeks and she mentally scolded herself for not slipping on her shoes before she'd answered the door. But it was a warm May afternoon and certainly pleasant enough in the house to go without footwear.

You're reacting like a foolish teenager, Mariah. Finn doesn't find anything fascinating about your pink toenails. And he hasn't come to Stallion Canyon to ogle you in any form or fashion. He's here because of Harry and no other reason.

Clearing her throat, she blocked out the scolding voice in her head and tried to form a sensible question. "So you're saying you want Harry to be your son?"

To her relief, his gaze returned to Harry and as he studied the child, she could see something that looked an awfully lot like love move over his features. The sight smacked Mariah right in the middle of her heart. A man was supposed to care that much for his child, she thought. Yet a part of her had been hoping Finn would be the irresponsible type. That he'd gladly hand the responsibility of raising Harry over to her. But it was becoming clear that he had no intention of stepping aside. So where was that going to leave her?

He said, "This wasn't the way I'd planned on becoming a father. But now that I have Harry in my arms, it feels right and good."

She folded her hands together atop her lap and tried to keep the confused emotions swirling inside her from showing on her face.

"So you believe he's actually your son?" she asked guardedly.

"I do. I think you'd have to agree that he takes after me. The red in his hair and dimples in his cheeks."

"Maybe. But that's hardly proof."

Frowning, he moved closer to where she sat, and Mariah instinctively placed a hand on each arm of the rocker and both feet flat on the floor.

"Something in your voice says you're hoping I won't be the father," he said tersely.

A blush scalded her cheeks. "I only want what's best for Harry."

He eyed her with cool conviction. "I don't know what sort of man you think I am, Ms. Montgomery, but—"

"Please, call me Mariah," she interrupted. "Calling me Ms. Montgomery makes me feel like I'm in the classroom."

Distracted now, he latched onto her last word. "Classroom? You're a teacher?"

"High school. History. That surprises you?"

Confusion flitted across his rugged face. "Aimee insinuated that Stallion Canyon was a profitable horse ranch. I just assumed the ranch was your livelihood, too."

A dead weight sank to the pit of her stomach as she slowly pushed herself out of the rocker. "I'll explain in the kitchen. It's time for Harry's bottle and I'm sure you could do with some coffee or something."

"Coffee sounds good," he agreed. "Lead the way."

With the baby cuddled safely against his chest, Finn followed Mariah out of the nursery and down a hallway that eventually intersected a small breezeway. Once there, she turned left down another short hallway until they reached a wide arched opening.

"We used to have a cook, but we had to let her go," she tossed over her shoulder. "Hopefully, you can tolerate my coffee-making."

They stepped into a rectangle-shaped kitchen with a ceiling opened to the rafters and a floor covered with ceramic tile patterned in dark blues and greens. To the right side of the room a round oak table and chairs were positioned near a group of wide windows covered with sheer blue curtains. To the left, white wooden cabinets with glass doors lined two whole walls, while a large work island also served as a breakfast bar.

Glancing over her shoulder, she said, "Have a seat at the bar or the table. Wherever you'd like. I'll get the coffee going, then heat Harry's bottle."

Since he was closer to the bar, Finn sank onto one of the padded stools and propped the baby in a comfortable upright position against his left arm. So far the tot seemed to be a good-natured boy. He hadn't yet let out a cry or even a fussy whine, but living in the same house with Rafe's two children, Colleen and Austin, had taught Finn that a baby's demeanor could change in an instant.

"What was wrong with the cook?" he asked curiously. "Burned the food?"

Greta, their family cook back on the Silver Horn Ranch, had been with them for more than thirty years. He couldn't imagine anyone but her making their meals and ruling the kitchen.

Over at the cabinet counter, Mariah was busy pouring water into a coffeemaker. He was still trying to grasp the fact that she was a teacher. Apparently, being in a classroom full of kids was a more comfortable job to her than sitting atop a horse.

You're wondering too much about the woman, Finn. It doesn't matter what she does for a living or for fun. Once you take Harry away from here, you probably won't see her again. Unless she comes to the Horn to visit Harry from time to time.

Was that the way it was going to be? Finn asked himself. Was it already settled in Finn's mind that Harry belonged to him? That the baby belonged on the Silver Horn with him?

Mariah's voice suddenly interrupted the heavy questions pushing through his thoughts.

"Cora was a great cook. She'd worked here for years. But after Dad died, money got tight. We had to start cutting corners."

There was an embittered tone to her voice. One that shouldn't belong to someone so young and pretty, he decided. Sure, she'd obviously had to deal with her fair share of raw deals. But that didn't mean she needed to keep dragging those disappointments behind her.

"Aimee talked about your father passing away," he told her. "I could see she was still pretty cut up about his death."

"Aimee and Dad were very close. She was just like him—obsessed with horses. Especially the wild ones," she added bluntly.

Was Mariah trying to say that Aimee had possessed a wild streak? Had Aimee shared her bed with Finn because she'd liked living recklessly? Or had she, as Mariah had implied, used him to get pregnant? Whatever the reason, it was clear that Aimee hadn't been completely honest with him, and that left Finn feeling like a fool for ever getting involved with her in the first place.

The baby let out a short cry and Finn looked down to see that the child was gnawing on his fist. "Harry, you must be hungry or teething," he said to the boy.

Finn's voice caught the baby's attention and Harry went quiet as he stared curiously up at him. Finn used the moment to touch his forefinger to the baby's hand, and instantly the tiny fingers latched tightly around his. Harry's response filled Finn with a fierce love and protection he'd never experienced before. Father or not, the baby needed him.

As another thought suddenly struck him, he glanced over to where Mariah was gathering mugs from the cabinet. "Do you have a copy of Harry's birth certificate?"

"I have the original. It's safely stored with my important documents. Harry's name is registered as Harrison Ray Calhoun—the Ray being our father's name." She turned a pointed look on him. "So where do we go from here? A DNA test?"

He'd been waiting for her to say those three little letters. The birth certificate stated Finn as the father, but Mariah wasn't yet ready to accept that as complete validation. And perhaps she was right. After all, a child's parentage was a serious matter. Yet seeing Harry and holding the little guy in his arms had caused some kind of upheaval inside Finn.

He didn't understand what had come over him. All he knew was that this child had suddenly become everything to him. The idea that a clinical test could say otherwise chilled Finn to the very bottom of his being.

"I suppose that would be the logical thing to do. That way his parentage would never be in doubt," Finn said

with slow thoughtfulness. "I just wish it wasn't necessary. I don't want Harry to grow up and learn that the
identity of his father was ever in question."

Forgetting her task, she walked over and placed a
hand on Harry's back. "I don't necessarily want that for
him, either. But I want him to have the 'right' father."

He slanted her a wry look. "Don't you mean you want
him to have the right 'parent'?"

Her long black lashes lowered and partially hid the
thoughts flickering in her gray eyes.

"What do you mean?"

The threads of his patience were quickly snapping.
"Don't act clueless. You want to keep Harry for yourself.
You're hoping like hell that I won't be the father."

Her mouth fell open. "I never said that."

"You didn't have to. I can see it all over your face.
Hear it in your voice."

Shaking her head, she turned her back to him. "If
that were true, then why did I call you? I didn't have to,
you know," she said, her voice heavy with resentment.
"I could've kept Harry all to myself."

He instinctively cradled the baby closer to his chest.
"Yeah, you could've left me in the dark. But then you
couldn't have lived with your conscience. Or with Harry,
once he grew old enough to start asking about his father.
You'd have to make up a lie to tell him why you didn't
make an effort to contact me. Then one lie starts leading to another. You're not that kind of woman. The kind
that can live on a bed of lies."

She whirled around to face him and Finn was struck
by the moisture collecting in her eyes. He didn't want
to hurt this black-haired beauty. She'd already been hurt

enough. But she needed to understand that he wasn't a fool. Or at the mercy of her wants and wishes.

"You don't know what kind of person I am! We've only just met." A sneer twisted her lips as she raked a disapproving gaze over him. "But then I need to remember you jumped into bed with Aimee right after you met her. I suppose you thought you knew her, too!"

His jaw tight, he said, "Your crude observations don't embarrass me, Mariah. But they do have me wondering. Maybe *you'd* like an invitation into my bed."

Her eyes widened with disbelief, then turned to cold steel. "That's the most insulting, despicable thing I've ever heard!"

"Is it?" he asked softly.

A scarlet blush crept over her face. "Look, Mr. Calhoun, the only thing you need to concern yourself with is the result of Harry's DNA test. And the faster we can get those done, the happier I'll be!"

Chapter Two

Finn watched Mariah stalk to the opposite end of the kitchen and thump a pair of empty mugs onto a plastic tray. He'd never spoken that way to any woman before and he wasn't quite sure what had prompted such a thing to come out of his mouth. Except that ever since he'd arrived on this ranch, she'd been subtly goading him. As though she considered it okay for her to judge him as a cad for having a romantic interlude with Aimee. As if she were infallible and would never stoop to such human impulses.

With a heavy sigh, he rose to his feet and walked over to where she was pulling a baby bottle filled with formula from the refrigerator. After giving him a cursory glance, she shut the door on the appliance and moved over to a microwave. Finn felt compelled to follow.

"I'm sorry, Mariah," he told her. "I shouldn't have said that to you. I was way out of line."

While the microwave whirred, she kept her back to him. It wasn't until the bell dinged that she retrieved the bottle, then turned to face him.

"Then why did you say it?" she asked stiffly.

The icy stare she'd stabbed him with earlier was gone. Now her gray eyes were dark with shadows, and Finn realized his question had touched far more than just her female pride. The notion made him feel even worse.

"Because you seemed set on judging me for spending a weekend with Aimee. That's not— Well, for your information, I don't go around having affairs, short or long, on a regular basis! Yet you want to make me out as a cad. What's the matter with you? Are you a prude or something?"

Outrage popped her mouth open and Finn expected her to flounce off in huff. But after a moment, her shoulders sagged and she glanced away. "Making a baby is a serious thing," she murmured.

She was avoiding his question, but he was hardly going to point that out to her now, Finn decided. Besides, he had the feeling that before this ordeal with Harry was finished, he was going to find out plenty about Mariah Montgomery.

"That's why I'm here," he said curtly. "Because there is a baby. A baby who's lost his mother."

She reached for Harry then, but Finn continued to hold him firmly against his chest. "Give me the bottle. I'd like to feed my son."

Her chin came up to a challenging angle. "It's yet to be determined whether Harry is your child, Mr. Calhoun."

"You decided that. I didn't. I agreed to a DNA test because you wanted one and my family back home wants one. But as far as I'm concerned, Harry has Calhoun blood running through his veins. And by the way," he added, "call me Finn. When you say Mr. Calhoun you make me think you're addressing my grandfather."

"All right, Finn. I guess I should appreciate your frankness. At least I'm not in the dark about where you stand with Harry."

She handed him the bottle. Finn carried it and the baby back over to the breakfast bar. After he'd taken a seat on one of the stools, he cradled Harry in a comfortable position in the crook of his left arm and offered him the warm bottle.

"Here's your dinner, little one," he told the baby. "Go for it."

The infant latched onto the nipple with a hunger that brought a faint smile to Finn's lips. Oh, what a stir this little guy was going to make on the Silver Horn, he thought. Especially with his grandfather Bart, who was all for the expansion of the Calhoun family.

He looked up as Mariah approached the bar carrying a tray with the coffee and containers of cream and sugar. As she placed it a safe distance from his elbow, she asked, "Would you like cream or sugar? Since you have your hands full, I can fix it for you."

"Just black. Thanks," he said, grateful that she was being somewhat hospitable. Especially after that sexual taunt about inviting her into his bed. No telling what she was thinking about him now. Her impression of him had most likely slipped from cad to pervert. But why her opinion of him should matter, he didn't know. Except that something about Mariah Montgomery got under his skin. He wanted to see approval in her eyes and a smile on those lovely lips.

Cradling one of the mugs with both hands, she stood a couple of steps away, watching Harry feed. After a long stretch of silence, she asked, "Where did a bachelor like you learn how to feed a baby?"

"My sister, Sassy, has two kids. A son, J.J., and a daughter, Skyler, born three months ago. And two of my brothers have small children."

"Playing with your little nieces and nephews is not the same as actually caring for them," she said bluntly.

Defending himself to this woman was definitely getting old, Finn thought, but he was going to do his best not to let his impatience show. Sparring with her wouldn't help matters. "I've done more than just play with them," he informed her. "I've babysat Sassy's kids while she and her husband went out for the evening. So I know about bottles and diapers and those sorts of things."

"You, a babysitter? That's hard to imagine."

Ignoring that jab, he said, "Sassy trusts me to care for her kids like they're my own. And I'm glad to do it for her."

"So the two of you are close," she said thoughtfully. "Aimee and I were that way once. But time and...other things caused us to grow apart."

The contents of the bottle had lowered to the point where Finn was forced to tilt it higher so Harry would ingest formula rather than air. She watched him make the adjustment, then seemingly satisfied that he knew how to feed a baby, she took a seat on the stool next to his.

Using his free hand, Finn reached for the mug of coffee, then carefully leaned his head away from Harry to take a sip. The brew was stronger than what he was normally used to, but it tasted good. The long drive up here, coupled with the stress of meeting Mariah and the baby, had worn him down.

After downing several sips of the coffee, he asked, "Do you have any other relatives living close by?"

"No. Our parents divorced when Aimee and I were small, and ever since, our mother has lived in Florida near her parents."

"Do any of them ever come to visit?"

A bitterness twisted her features. "Not hardly. Aimee and I were lucky to get a birthday or Christmas card from any of them. Now that I'm the only one left, it'll be easy for them to forget they have family back here on a dusty ranch."

So Mariah clearly wouldn't be getting any emotional support from that branch of the family. The idea bothered him greatly. Mariah was so young. She needed someone to embrace and encourage her through the loss of her sister and the transition it was making on her life. She needed a loving family surrounding her. But she had none.

He said, "I guess you can tell that Aimee didn't share much about her family life with me. But to be fair I didn't ask her a lot of personal questions. We mostly talked about horses and the things we had in common. I thought we'd have plenty of time for family talk later. I never believed…well, that things would end up like this."

Over the rim of her mug, she regarded him solemnly. "After you left Reno did you ever try to contact her?"

"Sure. I called several times. But the phone signal would break or she'd never answer. I even left messages on her voice mail, but she never returned them. I finally decided she wanted to put our weekend behind her. So I did the same."

She turned her head away and Finn could hear a heavy sigh swoosh out of her.

"I should apologize to you, too, Finn. You were right. I wanted to think of you as a cad. I'd made up my mind even before you arrived that you were the one who'd left Aimee in the lurch. That was easier than thinking my sister was…callous or indifferent or—" Her head swung back and forth. "Guess it doesn't matter now."

Aimee's true intentions toward Finn or her baby had died with her. And none of it could change the future now, Finn thought—unless the DNA test proved some other man had fathered Harry. But already his mind was balking at that idea. Something deep within him recognized that Harry was his child.

He glanced down to see that the baby was sound asleep, his lips slack around the nipple. Carefully, he eased the bottle from the boy's mouth and placed it on the bar.

"You don't need to apologize," he told Mariah. "We're both in the dark about each other and Aimee and how Harry came to be.

"So you don't have any other relatives around who could help you with the ranch? What about your dad's parents?" he asked.

She shook her head. "They died a few years ago within a few months of each other. Both had struggled with serious health problems."

"Sorry to hear that," he said gently.

Her sigh was wistful. "Aimee and I adored them both. After our parents divorced we lived with them for a while, then Dad purchased this ranch and the three of us moved up here. Having Stallion Canyon was his dream come true."

Finn glanced thoughtfully around the warm kitchen and tried to imagine what it had been like when her father and sister had been living. Had the three of them gathered at the dinner table and talked about their dreams and plans? Had there been jokes and laughter or arguments and worries?

"So this house—this ranch has been your home for many years," he stated the obvious.

Rising from the bar stool, she walked over to the cabinet and poured more coffee into her mug. "Since I was eight. And I'm twenty-eight now. So yes, this has been home for all my adult life. But not much longer," she added dully.

"So you're planning on moving?" he asked.

She said, "As soon as the real estate agent can sell the ranch."

There was a hollow sound to her voice, as though moving from this home had no effect on her. Finn didn't understand why the notion should bother him, but it did. A family ranch with a long history represented pride and hard work. It meant passing a home and legacy from one generation to the next. Had Mariah stopped to think of that, or was getting away from here more important? After twenty years she was bound to have deep roots and sentimental ties to the place. Could she be putting up a front? Pretending to him and even herself that it didn't matter where she lived?

"You're going to sell it? Damn, that's pretty final, isn't it?"

Glancing over her shoulder, she frowned at him. "I'm a teacher. Dad and Aimee are gone and I have no use for the land, the barns or the equipment. I've already gotten rid of all but ten of the horses. And I only have those because I can't find buyers. One of them is a prize stallion and I was holding out for a better price, but I'm almost to the point of giving him and the rest away. Cutting out the feed bill would help stop the ranch from sinking into deeper debt."

One thing he'd learned about Aimee during their brief time together was that Stallion Canyon and its horses had meant everything to her. But apparently Mariah didn't feel any such pull. Had it always been that way? he wondered. Or had hard times embittered her?

"My mistake," he said. "When I drove up earlier, I thought I saw a man at one of the barns. I assumed the ranch was doing business."

"That was Ringo," she explained. "He comes by twice a week to haul in feed and generally check on things. To save money I take care of the daily feeding."

Harry was the only reason Finn had traveled up here to Stallion Canyon. The ranch's financial condition, or its lone proprietor, was none of his business. But little by little Mariah was somehow drawing him into this place and her plight.

"Am I understanding you right, Mariah? You're selling the ranch because it's going under?"

She returned to her seat at the bar. "You're asking some very personal questions," she said.

Their gazes connected, and as he studied her gray eyes, he felt something stir in him. The sensation had nothing to do with the baby in his arms and everything to do with the moist gleam on her dusky lips and the subtle scent of flowers drifting to his nostrils.

Hellfire, what's wrong with you, Finn? One Montgomery sister has already had your baby. Now you're looking at this one as though you'd like to try for a second!

Trying to shake away the accusing voice in his head, he countered, "You've been telling me some very personal things."

She drew in a deep breath and his gaze instinctively fell to the rise and fall of her breasts. The gentle curves beneath the red checked blouse were just enough to fill a man's hands, he mentally gauged, or comfort a crying baby.

She said, "Normally I keep such things to myself. But if you are really Harry's father, then you need to hear about his mother's side of the family. As for me selling the ranch, I shouldn't have brought that up."

Finn's gaze roamed over her delicate features and crow-black hair. She was hardly the glamorous sort, but there was a sweet sort of sexiness about her that he found very hard to resist.

"Aimee told me your father died suddenly of a heart attack. There are five of us Calhoun brothers and we lost our mother about nine years ago to an accident. It's hell to lose someone you love."

She stared at the liquid inside her cup, and Finn got the impression she was purposely trying to keep from connecting with him in a personal way. Maybe the sight of him reminded her of Aimee. Or maybe she saw him as the villain, here to take Harry away from her. The idea made him feel like a jerk.

"At least you had a big family to support you. But I'm surviving. And I'm determined to move on with my life."

Over the years Finn and his family had dealt with troubles and sorrows, but they'd always had one another to lean on. Mariah had been facing everything on her own. He couldn't imagine how that felt, or what it would do to his spirit.

"I guess losing your father threw the ranch into up-heaval," he spoke his thoughts out loud.

Her expression rueful, she said, "That was the be-ginning of the downfall. After we buried Dad, Aimee promised she could keep Stallion Canyon profitable. And in the beginning I trusted her. She was a very good trainer. As good as Dad."

"At Reno I could see how competent Aimee was with her mustang. Your horses should've been bringing in top dollars. What happened?"

Mariah released a heavy sigh. "At first she worked very hard. And back then she had capable assistants to help her. But something caused her to change. She started spending money on frivolous things and ignor-ing her work. I tried to be patient, because I knew how much she was hurting over Dad's death. Each morning she walked out to the barns, she had to deal with work-ing without him. On top of that, her relationship with Bryce was going nowhere. Then she got pregnant. After that the ranch quickly went downhill."

Listening to Mariah now, it sounded as though Aimee had been a troubled soul long before he'd met her. Yet he hadn't glimpsed that side of her. All he'd seen was her laughter and smiles. The realization proved that he'd misjudged her badly. Did that mean any woman could fool him? Even this one?

"I suppose you're thinking I'm partly to blame for your problems," he said ruefully.

"I can't blame you for the choices Aimee made. And anyway, you might not be the man who got Aimee preg-nant."

So she was going to hold on to that notion, he thought

grimly. Well, he supposed she had that right. Just as much as he had the right to believe Harry was his son.

The thought had him looking down at the boy in his arms. The child was so tiny and vulnerable, so precious. He wanted to hold the sleeping baby's face next to his own, to breathe in his sweet scent and let the wonder of being a father settle deep inside him. He might have been gullible with Aimee, but he wasn't about to let Mariah dupe him. Especially when it came to Harry's parentage.

But what if Harry's DNA doesn't match yours, Finn? You'll have no argument to keep the boy. Maybe you ought to ask yourself if you're playing a fool's game.

Silently cursing the voice of warning in his head, he looked up to see Mariah's attention fixed on a nearby window. As he studied her pensive profile, he wondered if there was a special man in her life. Even though she wasn't married, there was still the possibility she had a boyfriend or fiancé. For all he knew, she might even have ideas of marrying and keeping Harry as her child.

Crazy or not, the mere idea of losing the baby in his arms left him cold inside. It changed the whole landscape of the future he'd been mentally painting for himself and his son. Harry gave him a purpose that he'd never had before, and he liked it.

"I believe I am that man," Finn said. "Aimee put my name on Harry's birth certificate. She did that for some reason. I only wish she'd contacted me. I could've helped—before things here on the ranch started falling apart."

She glanced at him, her expression wry. "We needed help all right. About a month before her accident, we were forced to sell off part of the horses just to keep the bills paid. Seeing them go opened Aimee's eyes somewhat. But it was already too late."

Finn frowned with confusion. "If money was that tight, how did she get the money to go on a skiing holiday?"

"Two of Aimee's girlfriends paid for the trip. They were hoping a break from the baby and the ranch would help her get her head on straight. Now they blame themselves for her death."

"Do you blame them?"

Frowning, she looked at him. "No. Accidents can happen anywhere."

"You've never told me exactly how Aimee died. Do you believe it truly was an accident?"

The widening of her eyes told Finn his question had surprised her.

"Why, yes, I do. Her friends said that one minute they were all headed down the slope together and everything was fine. Then a steep embankment appeared several yards on down the path. One of the friends managed to swerve around it, but Aimee and the other girl chose to ski over it. Both of them ramped the ledge and fell on the other side. There was soft powder on the ground that day, but something about the twisted way she landed severed Aimee's spinal cord."

"I'm sorry," he said quietly. "But after all you've said about Aimee it got me to wondering if maybe she was depressed or wasn't herself and—well, that she was deliberately being reckless."

Her brows pulled together in a scowl. "I'd be the first to admit that Aimee liked to live on the edge. Most normal folks would be terrified to climb on a horse that had bucking on its mind. But my sister relished the challenge and excitement. Still, as for that day on the ski slope, no, I believe it was an accident. Nothing more."

Finn was thankful for that much, at least. He hated thinking the responsibility of mothering Harry and the weight of the floundering ranch had pushed Aimee to the point where she hadn't cared whether she lived or died.

Still, the facts of Aimee's accident didn't change what was happening to Mariah now. She was on the verge of losing everything, he thought bleakly. How was she going to pick herself up and start a new life without her home? Without Harry?

Shoving the troubling questions aside, he said, "Aimee's death. Harry being born. There's some reason it all happened. And no matter the circumstances of how he was brought into the world, just holding this little guy in my arms makes me feel like a blessed man."

She said nothing to that. Instead, she stared at him, her gaze frozen on his face. While Finn waited for her to say anything, silence stretched between them like a taut highline.

After several more moments passed without a response, he finally asked, "Is something wrong?"

She jumped to her feet and cleared her throat. "I'm sorry," she said, her voice choked. "Please excuse me."

Before Finn could react, she was rushing toward the arched doorway and as he watched her retreating back, he knew there were already tears on her face.

Damn it! Now what?

With a heavy sigh, he rose to his feet and carried the sleeping baby out of the kitchen and back to the nursery.

As soon as he walked into the room, he spotted Mariah standing by a window near the crib, gazing out at the rugged landscape in the distance. Was she thinking about leaving this ranch? No doubt everything about the place reminded her of her father and sister. Or was it the fear of losing Harry that had caused her to break down in tears?

Finn placed the baby in the crib and covered him with a light blanket. It wasn't until he straightened from the task that he noticed Mariah was looking over her shoulder at him. Thankfully, there were no tears on her face, but Finn didn't miss the redness of her eyes. The sight hit him far harder than it should have.

"I'm sorry for rushing away like that, Finn," she said huskily. "Everything suddenly piled up on me."

He moved from the side of the crib and went to stand next to her. "I hardly need an apology," he told her. "But it would be nice to see a smile on your face."

Turning slightly, she cast him a sidelong glance. "I'm not in a smiling mood," she admitted. "Harry is on my mind. I'm thinking this ranch should eventually be handed down to him. It should remain his home. But sooner rather than later it's going to belong to someone else. And if it turns out you're his father, then none of that will matter anyway. You'll be wanting him to live with you."

"That's my plan. If Harry is my son, then he's going home with me. The child belongs with his father."

Her mouth fell open, snapped shut, and opened again. "I can't let that happen, Finn."

A cool chill rushed through him. "Excuse me, but if DNA proves Harry is mine, then I have every right to take him."

Her expression bleak, she turned her back to him. "Okay, I'll admit that as his father you'd have the right. But that's not all there is to it," she said in a low tone. "I

mean, Harry is used to me. I've been his mother since…
well, practically since he was born. To pull him away
from me would be traumatic for both of us. Besides, I
don't know anything about you. I wouldn't be much of
an aunt if I simply turned him over to you without learning who you are."

Finn's first instinct was to remind Mariah that he'd
already been robbed of the first few months of his son's
life because her sister had deliberately left him in the
dark. But now was not the time to get into a bitter battle
with her, he decided. It wouldn't help his cause to have
her thinking he was a hothead who had no business dealing with a baby. She'd learn soon enough that he was
Harry's father and that he wasn't about to allow her, or
anyone, to come between him and his son.

Drawing in a deep breath, he tried to remain cool
and collected. "I have all kinds of identification with
me. And if you'd like to call and speak with someone
about me or my family, I can give you plenty of character references."

Biting down on her lip, Mariah closed her eyes and
tried to calm the churning fear inside her. What could
she say? How could she make this man understand that
Harry was all she had left in the world? He was her little
boy. If Finn Calhoun took him away from her, she didn't
think she could bear the pain.

If the test revealed he was Harry's daddy, there'd be
no way she could prevent him from taking custody of
her baby—unless he was unfit to be a parent, and he
hardly looked that. This hunky cowboy looked like a
man who was in complete control of himself and everything around him.

Bracing herself with a deep breath, she turned back to him and was immediately struck again by his huge presence. She couldn't put her finger on it, but there was something about Finn that set him apart from the other cowboys who'd worked on Stallion Canyon. He had enough confidence for two men and the looks to go with it. But that wasn't exactly the reason her gaze kept returning to him. There was something about his blue eyes and the hard curve of his lips that invited her to draw near him. And that could prove to be dangerous.

With her mouth feeling as though she'd eaten a bowl of desert sand, she said, "I don't need a bunch of your friends mouthing your superlative qualities to me. I need to see for myself what sort of man you are."

His rusty brown brows pulled together in a frown while his keen gaze rambled lazily over her face, and Mariah suddenly wished she'd dressed that morning in a shirt that buttoned tightly at her throat and wrists. At least then she might not be feeling so downright naked.

After a long, pregnant pause, he said, "Most folks consider me a respectable, hardworking man. How do folks around here feel about you?"

For a moment she was taken aback. She hadn't been expecting him to turn the tables on her. "I have a few friends," she said. "And the school where I teach wants me back next year. Does that tell you anything about my reputation?"

A corner of his lips curved slightly upward and Mariah found she couldn't tear her eyes from the provocative image. How many women, besides Aimee, had felt the pleasure of those hard lips on hers? she wondered. Was he the kind of man that frequently pursued women in general, or did one in particular have to catch his attention before he went after her?

His low chuckle caressed her senses, and longing suddenly pierced the empty spots inside her. How nice it would be to hear his laugh each and every day, to be able to laugh with him. To feel his hands touching her, protecting her, loving her.

"You said you wanted to get to know me. Could be that I'd like to know more about you, too. Do you have a boyfriend? Or fiancé?"

Rattled even more by his questions, she moved around him and returned to the side of Harry's crib. He'd laid the baby on his back and tucked a lightweight blue blanket around him. The idea of the tall, tough cowboy caring so gently for the baby caused her eyes to mist over once again.

"No boyfriend. And definitely not a fiancé."

"And why is that? You don't want to be married?"

She made an indifferent shrug, even though a tangle of emotions was suddenly choking her. "I'm waiting for the right man to come along," she mumbled.

She wasn't about to add any more to her explanation. She hardly wanted him, or anyone else for that matter, to know that she'd never gotten over losing the only man she'd ever cared about to another woman. And considering the woman had been her sister, Mariah wasn't sure she'd ever get over the betrayal.

Slowly, she sensed his presence moving alongside her, and then the faint scent of him drifted to her nostrils. He smelled like a man who'd been bathed in desert wind and kissed by hot sunshine, and for one brief moment she wondered what it would be like to press her

nose against his throat, to breathe in that evocative scent.
To let herself forget that he'd once been Aimee's lover.

He said, "You must be waiting for Mr. Perfect."

The huskiness of his voice was such a sensual sound
it caused goose bumps to form on the backs of her arms.

"That's none of your business," she said.

"Probably not. But I'm a curious kind of guy. I've
been trying to figure out how a woman who looks like
you is living out here alone—without a man to care for
her. Protect her."

And make love to her. Mariah could hear the un-
spoken words in his voice as clearly as she could hear
Harry's soft breathing behind them.

The fragile grip she had on her senses was coming
close to snapping. "Aimee was always the one who wanted
a man in her life. Not me."

"That could change—if you met a man you couldn't
live without."

Everything inside Mariah had quickly gone hot and
shaky. And she wondered wildly how he would react if
she suddenly turned and placed her palms against his
chest. If she were to tilt her face up to his, would he
want to kiss her? Oh my. Oh my. Why were these crazy,
wicked thoughts going through her head? Why was he
making her forget that she was a practical woman?

"I'm just trying to survive, Finn. I'm not foolish
enough to believe a knight will come riding through here
on a big white horse and make all my troubles go away."

A wry grin tugged at his lips. "He might come riding through here on a big brown mustang. Ever think
that might happen?"

Her laugh was short and caustic. "If that ever happened I'd run him off with a loaded shotgun. Once these

last ten are gone, I never want to see another mustang. If it hadn't been for the wild horses I might have persuaded Aimee to get out of the business before we went broke. But she was obsessed with the damned things. And now—"

As her words trailed away, his hand wrapped gently around her upper arm, and the touch splintered her resolve to remain indifferent to him. Heat from his fingers was rushing to her cheeks, then plunging downward, showering her whole body with sparks.

"You're blaming the wrong thing for your troubles, Mariah. At one point, those horses were running free, caring for themselves. They didn't ask to be captured and confined."

Mariah's chin dropped against her chest. She sounded like a pouting child, blaming her problems on everything and everyone but herself. But grief, worry, anger and resentment had been playing with her emotions for so long now. And for just as long, she'd been trying to hide her emotions, to pretend that she was strong and unaffected. And now something about Finn was pulling her feelings right out in the open.

"Sorry. I'll admit my thinking is twisted. But Aimee refused to consider any other job. With her it was the horses or nothing. And that's where the ranch was headed—with nothing."

The subtle tightening of his fingers on her arm had her lifting her face up to his, and as her gaze probed the depths of his blue eyes, her heart thumped so hard she could feel it banging against her ribs.

"Look, Mariah, horses can get into a person's blood. Caring for them, working with them, loving them. It becomes sort of an addiction. One that's impossible to shake. Even when you know they're costing too much money or taking you down a wrong path."

"So you're saying your job has to involve horses or you wouldn't be happy?"

"I'd be miserable without horses around me."

Disappointment washed through her. Which was ridiculous. Finn's dreams and desires had nothing to do with her. Except where Harry was concerned. She didn't want the child to have a father like hers, who'd spent every weekend at horse shows and every waking minute of the day at the training barn.

"You and Aimee would have made a perfect pair," she said stiffly.

His gaze rambled over her face. "It takes more than a shared love of something to make a perfect partnership. The fact that Aimee wasn't interested in building a relationship with me proves that much."

She grimaced. "As far as men go, Aimee didn't know what she wanted."

"Thanks," he said with sarcasm.

Her gaze connected with his and Mariah's heart gave a hard thump. "Tell me, Finn, if you'd known about Aimee's pregnancy would you have married her?"

His expression didn't flinch, or his gaze break away from hers. "That's hard to say. Aimee might not have wanted marriage. And as it is, I'm not sure I would've wanted it, either. When I do marry I want it to be for love, not out of obligation."

"So you weren't in love with my sister?"

"There wasn't enough time for that. But who knows, if Aimee had given us a chance, we might've fallen in love and gotten married."

Hearing this sexy cowboy talk about loving and mar-

rying Aimee bothered her in more ways than she cared
to admit. Maybe because she'd never had a rugged man
like him give her a second glance. Not as long as Aimee
had been around to monopolize all the male attention.

"Then you'd be my brother-in-law right now. And a
widower."

"Yeah."

Mariah was so busy trying to read the emotions in his
eyes that long moments passed before she realized the
room had gone quiet and Finn's hand was still wrapped
around her arm.

*Move, Mariah. Step away from him before his touch
begins to feel too good to resist. Before your dreams
start down a very foolish path.*

"I—please—excuse me, Finn. I have to go."

Before she could let herself weaken, before he could
guess the longing on her face, Mariah pulled away from
him and raced out of the nursery. She didn't stop until
she was inside her bedroom with the door shut firmly
behind her. And by then she was trembling from head
to toe.

With her shoulders slumped against the door, she covered her hot face with both hands and sucked in several
deep breaths. She'd been through too much to let herself
break down now. She needed to show Finn that she was
a strong, capable woman. More than that, she needed
to convince herself that he was a man she couldn't fall
in love with.

Chapter Three

Finn sat at the kitchen table, his hands wrapped around a mug of half-burned coffee, as he tried to decide what to do next. He'd been sitting there for more than half an hour, waiting for Mariah to show her face again. Since she'd run from the nursery, he hadn't heard her stirring, and he was starting to wonder whether he should search her out and apologize, or tell her he was leaving for town.

Neither option appealed to him. He wasn't ready to leave the ranch just yet. Not until the two of them had made definite plans concerning Harry. And he hadn't done anything he needed to apologize for—except maybe make her face the reality of Harry's being a Calhoun.

Rising from the table, he walked over to a set of double windows and studied the view behind the house. From this spot, he could just make out a corner of one large barn, a smaller shed and a maze of connecting corrals. Except for a few birds and the wind twisting the leaves, nothing was moving. It was a sad and lonely sight, he thought grimly.

"I see you've helped yourself to the coffee. I'm glad. I haven't been a very good hostess."

He hadn't heard her enter the room, and the sound of her voice had him quickly turning to see her walking toward him. While she'd been in her room, she'd put on a pair of faded red cowboy boots and released her hair from its ponytail. Now the long black waves framed her face and rested on her shoulders. Her nose looked as though she'd patted it with a powder puff, while a sheen of pink glossed her lips. She looked sweet and sexy and totally unassuming. And as Finn stared at her, he felt a strange sensation slowing coursing through him. Was this how it felt to be mesmerized by a woman?

"I dug into your brownies, too," he told her. "They're good. Did you make them?"

A faint smile touched her lips. It was the first one that Finn had seen on her face and the sight encouraged him. Maybe the short break from him and the baby had put her in a better mood.

"Thanks. I like to bake and cook. Now that Cora is gone I get to do plenty of it."

"I've been listening for Harry. Does he usually cry when he wakes up?"

"Depends if he's wet or hungry. Most of the time he's a happy baby. I'll find him wide-awake just cooing and looking around." She walked over to the cabinet and dumped the last of the syrupy black coffee into the sink. "We had an intercom system put in after Harry was born. It was rather expensive. But I can go anywhere in the house or out on the porches and still be able to hear every little sound he makes."

"Dad had one installed in the ranch house years ago. It was rarely used until Rafe and Lilly had their babies. That's my brother and sister-in-law. They have two kids. A girl, Colleen. And a boy, Austin. He's just a few months older than Harry."

She looked at him with interest. "So Harry would have cousins to play with. That is, if he truly is a Calhoun."

Obviously she was going to point out the question of Harry's parentage at every turn of their conversation, he thought drearily. Well, if it made her feel better, then so be it. She'd have her bubble busted soon enough.

"Six little cousins. The Calhoun family is big. And I don't figure it's quit growing yet."

"Hmm. Must be nice. To be in a big family. I wouldn't know." She rinsed out the coffee carafe, then placed it back on the warmer. "So tell me about yourself and your family. What do you do back in Nevada?"

Rising to his feet, he carried his cup over to where she stood, then rested his hip against the cabinet counter. "I manage the horse division of the Silver Horn Ranch. Along with the cattle, we raise quarter horses for show, cutting and ranch use."

Mariah stared at him while trying not to appear shocked. Aimee had simply told her that Finn was a horseman and Mariah had presumed he'd worked as a wrangler for some ranch, or was simply a guy who liked horses. Aimee had never mentioned anything as impressive as the manager of a horse division.

Her head swung back and forth. "We? Uh—you have other men helping you?"

"Why, yes. I thought—" Tilting his head to one side, he studied her. "Apparently Aimee didn't tell you that my home is the Silver Horn."

Confused now, she said, "No. She didn't. And I'm not familiar with that name. Should I be?"

Her question put a look of amused disbelief on his face.

"Most folks on both sides of the state line have heard of the Silver Horn. But with Aimee gone and Stallion Canyon up for sale I guess you don't keep up with ranching news."

As long as her father had been alive, Mariah had been proud of Stallion Canyon. Ray Montgomery had poured his heart and soul into the land and the horses, and along the way had provided his daughters with a good home and security. But once he'd died, everything had taken a downhill slide. As the burden of debt had grown heavier on Mariah's shoulders, she'd started to resent the place that had been her home for twenty years. Yet now, hearing Finn speak as though the ranch was done and finished left a hollowness inside her.

Resting her hand on the cabinet counter, she turned so that she was facing him. "So this Silver Horn where you work—it's a big outfit?"

He nodded. "I don't just work there. I live there, too. It belongs to the Calhoun family. My great-grandfather started it many years ago. These days my grandfather Bart—I call him Gramps—is the director of the whole shebang. We run a few thousand head of cattle and usually have two to three hundred horses on hand."

Mariah was stunned. Why had Aimee kept something like that from her? Had her sister gone after Finn because she'd known he was wealthy, then later changed her mind about pursuing a relationship with him? Dear Lord, it was all so strange, so mind-boggling.

She tried not to sound as dazed as she felt. "Your ranch must cover a lot of acreage."

"We own several thousand acres and lease that much more from the BLM—the Bureau of Land Management," he told her.

Mariah felt like a fool. Not only because Aimee had kept her in the dark, but because she hadn't looked into Finn's background before she'd called to tell him about Harry. At least she would've known what sort of man she'd be facing. But then, a man's material worth didn't necessarily speak for his character, she reasoned. And she was quickly learning that Finn wasn't a man who could be summed up in one short visit.

"I apologize if my questions sound stupid. But Aimee didn't tell me anything about you. Except that you lived in Nevada and liked horses."

He shrugged. "Guess that was all that mattered to her. When I told her I lived on the Silver Horn, she seemed to be familiar with the ranch. But we didn't talk about it that much. She asked about our remuda and the brood-mares and a little about the ranch house. It didn't seem important to her."

Her thoughts whirled as she gathered the few dirty dishes scattered over the countertop and piled them into the sink. "So Aimee understood you were wealthy?"

"I figure she made that assumption. But I never told her any such thing. Only a braggart starts spouting off information like that to a woman he's just met," he said.

"I don't expect you share the balance of your bank account with the men you meet."

Pulling back her shoulders, she said, "I don't meet that many men. But if I did, they wouldn't hear about my finances. I just wondered…"

"If Aimee pursued me because of my wealth?" he asked wryly. "I think the fact that she didn't attempt to continue our relationship tells you how much she appreciated my money."

Mariah thoughtfully swiped a soapy sponge slowly over a saucer. "I don't mean to pry, Finn. I'm just trying to understand why my sister put off contacting you about Harry. Could be she was worried about you getting custody—since you could provide more financial security for him. Far more than she ever could. But that doesn't make much sense, either. Because she wasn't afraid to put your name on the birth certificate."

He moved a step closer and Mariah's nerves twisted even tighter.

"I don't think you ought to be worrying over Aimee's motives anymore," he said. "Harry's future is the main issue now. And that brings us to the DNA test. Do you think we can get that taken care of tomorrow?"

Her throat went tight as she glanced over at him. "You're not wanting to waste any time, are you?"

"Dallying around won't tell us anything. And my job on the Horn is—well, pretty demanding. I need to get back there as soon as possible."

"I suppose I can call the school and let them know I need to take a couple hours off in the morning. Long enough for us to go to the health department and get the samples taken," she said guardedly. "That way you can go on back to Nevada. And receive the results in the mail."

"That isn't going to happen."

His instant retort had her dropping the sponge and squaring around to face him. "What does that mean?"

"It means I'm not about to leave here without Harry."

The determination in his voice sent a chill slithering down her spine. "And what if you're not his father? All that waiting will be wasted."

His clear blue gaze traveled over her face in a way that made Mariah forget about breathing.

"Let me be the judge of that," he said quietly.

Shoving a hand in her hair, she pushed it off her forehead, while silently yelling at her heart to slow down. Otherwise, she was going to faint right at his feet.

Drawing in a steadying breath, she said, "You must be feeling confident that Harry is your child."

"I am. And deep down you believe I'm his father, too. Don't you?"

Clamping her jaw tight, she was determined not to let him see her cry, to let him know that the thought of losing Harry was shattering her whole being.

Turning back to the sink full of dishes, she picked up the sponge and twisted it until soapy foam covered both hands. "I'll believe what the DNA test says," she said hoarsely. "Nothing less."

She was fighting back tears when she felt him move behind her and place his hand on her shoulder. Mariah squeezed her eyes shut as heat raced up the side of her neck and down her arm.

"Mariah," he said gently, "I'm not an ogre. I can see how much you love Harry. But a man who could leave his son—well, he wouldn't be much of a man. Would he?"

Swallowing hard, she turned to face him, but the moment her gaze met his, her self-control crumbled and she began pounding her fist against his chest. "No, damn you! I wished I'd never called you! I'd have my baby and you'd never know the difference!"

By the time he grabbed her flying fists and anchored them tightly against his chest, she was sobbing, her cheeks drenched with tears. But what this man thought about her no longer mattered. All she cared about was Harry.

"Hush, Mariah. Please, don't cry."

He gently drew her forward, until her wet cheek was pressed against the middle of his chest and his hand was stroking the back of her head.

Even if Mariah had wanted to resist, the solid comfort of his arms, the tender touch of his fingers upon her hair, was a balm to her raw nerves. A man hadn't touched her this way in ages. She hadn't wanted one to touch her. Until now.

Eventually, the warmth of his arms eased the chill inside her and dried the tears in her eyes. By then, his masculine scent and the hard muscle beneath her cheek were turning her thoughts in a totally different direction.

He murmured against the top of her head. "Better now?"

The husky note in his voice shivered through her like a cold drink on a hot day. So good. So perfect. But she couldn't keep standing here in his arms, letting her erotic thoughts get out of control.

Quickly, she stepped back from his tempting body and wiped fingers against the traces of tears on her cheeks.

"Forgive me," she whispered. "I'm behaving like a

shrew. But I—" Her gaze met his and her heart very nearly stopped as she spotted a sensual gleam in his blue eyes. Had the embrace they'd just shared affected him, too? Or were her scattered senses making her see things that weren't really there?

His lips took on a wry slant. "Forget it, Mariah. I can take a few punches. Besides, you made your point. You chose to call me. Otherwise I wouldn't have known anything about Harry. Unless by some chance I ran across some of her old friends at a horse show, and even then, I probably wouldn't have made the connection of me being her child's father."

His expression softened. "I'm grateful that you made that call, Mariah. Even though I understand how much it's breaking your heart."

Blinking at a fresh wave of tears, she turned back to the sink and thrust her hands into the water. Better there than pounding them against Finn's chest and making a complete neurotic fool of herself, she thought dismally.

A shaky breath shuddered past her lips. "Harry deserves a father," she said bluntly.

He moved a few steps away and Mariah went limp with relief. For the first time in her life, she couldn't trust herself near a man.

"The afternoon is getting late," he said, "and I haven't gotten a room in town yet. Can you recommend a good place to stay?"

She glanced over her shoulder at him and suddenly without warning, she heard herself saying, "You don't need to drive back to town. You're welcome to stay here. There are plenty of empty bedrooms and you'd be close to Harry."

And to me.

The voice in her head came out of the blue. Just as her unplanned invitation had come from a place inside her she hadn't known existed. Dear Lord, she must be cracking up. Earlier, she'd wanted rid of this man. Now she wanted to get closer to him. This cowboy was putting some sort of hypnotic spell on her.

"It's nice of you to offer, Mariah, but I don't expect you to put me up for the night."

The arch of his brows said her invitation had surprised him. But it couldn't have surprised him any more than it had her.

"Dad would've already insisted you be our guest," she reasoned. "I wouldn't feel right doing any less."

"But you live here alone."

She frowned. "What's that got to do with it?"

"I wouldn't want to make you feel uncomfortable."

Heat rushed to her cheeks. "I trust you to be a gentleman. And you look like a strong guy—you can help me with the barn chores."

The broad smile he gave her was like a dazzling ray of sunshine. It warmed Mariah as nothing had in a long time.

"You just got yourself a ranch hand and a houseguest. Thank you, Mariah."

She inclined her head in agreement. "If you'd like to fetch your things, I'll show you where to put them."

"I'll be right back," he promised.

Once he was gone from the room, Mariah leaned weakly against the cabinet and wondered if she just made the biggest mistake of her life. Opening her home to Finn wasn't going to make him change his mind about taking Harry.

Oh, come on, Mariah. Inviting him to stay here on

the ranch had nothing to do with Harry. You want him around because looking at him is a constant thrill. Hearing his voice shivers over your senses like sweet, slow music. And touching him made your whole body ache for more.

Disgusted with the mocking voice in her head, Mariah left the kitchen and hurried toward the block of bedrooms located at the back of the house. As she collected clean linen for Finn's bed, she assured herself that she wasn't about to be charmed by the Nevada horseman. She had more important and pressing issues in her life to deal with. Like finding out whether Finn actually was Harry's father.

Later that evening, Finn stood in the middle of the ranch yard, surveying the barns and surrounding landscape. From what he could see from his limited view, the ranch was a beautiful property. Run-down in places, but still very usable.

Not far to the east of the barns and corrals, forest-covered mountains formed a towering green wall. To the west, the land swept away to an open valley floor dotted with a mixture of hardwoods and evergreens. Some twenty to thirty miles beyond the valley, tall blue mountains etched a ragged horizon against the sky. Stallion Canyon was a much greener land than that of the Horn, and the beauty of it made Finn long to straddle a horse and explore the foothills and meandering streams.

He wondered if Mariah ever had the urge to ride over the ranch, or had the financial difficulties she'd been under robbed all pleasures she'd taken from the place?

Damn it, he wished he could quit thinking about the woman. Quit wondering why she'd invited him to stay here on Stallion Canyon. Especially when his presence only seemed to upset her.

You didn't have to accept her invitation, Finn. You could have told her a quick "no thank you." Instead, you couldn't accept fast enough. So you could be near Harry, you told yourself. Bull. Admit it, you want to be near Mariah, too.

Fighting away the condemning voice in his head, he walked over to a long shed row running the length of a large red barn. A black stallion was hanging his head over a stall gate, and Finn was instantly drawn to the horse.

"Hey there, handsome guy," he greeted the animal. "I'll bet you'd like it if I got you out of there, wouldn't you?"

The horse nudged his nose against Finn's hand and he obliged the animal by gently stroking his face. After a moment, Finn moved his hand on down the strong, arched neck. There, beneath the long curtain of black mane, he found the alpha angles of a BLM freeze brand, which was made by freezing a copper iron with liquid nitrogen before pressing it to the animal's hide. The process turned the hair on the horse white, rather than burning it off. The white symbols the BLM used could be translated to reveal what state the horse had originally come from, its age, and its own individual code number.

The sight of the markings against the horse's black coat tugged at something deep within Finn. The stallion had once run wild and free over the mountains and plains. Most likely he'd had his own harem of mares and had fought valiantly to keep his family safely at his side.

Now this majestic animal was confined behind fences, and though he was getting more nutrition and care than he could've ever possibly obtained out on the range, Finn would love to see him running free on miles of grazing land, with a band of mares racing close behind him.

The image brought back all the arguments he'd had in the past with his father and grandfather over the mustangs. For three or more years now, Finn had fought to incorporate wild horses into the breeding program on the Silver Horn, but Orin and Bart had strongly resisted.

Now that Finn was standing face-to-face with this regal animal, his determination to work with a herd of mustangs grew even stronger. Sooner than later, he was going to take a stand for what he wanted. And he wasn't going to back down.

The ring of his cell interrupted his thoughts and he reluctantly pulled the instrument from a leather holder fastened to his belt.

"Hi, Dad," he greeted. "What's up?"

"I've been ringing your phone for the past two hours! We've been sitting on pins and needles back here waiting to hear from you!"

"Sorry. These past few hours have been like a roller coaster. I've just now gotten a chance to grab a quiet moment."

Orin said, "You sound exhausted."

Finn's gaze drifted away from a pen of mares and over to the house. Seeing Harry for the first time and dealing with Mariah's emotional reactions had done something to him. He wasn't the same man who'd driven away from the Silver Horn Ranch early this morning. But trying to explain that to his father would sound ridiculous.

"It's not every day that a man sees his son for the first time. A son he didn't know he had."

A long pause followed, then Orin said, "Sounds like

you've made up your mind pretty damn quick about this baby."

"The boy resembles me, Dad. His hair is auburn and curly. And he has my dimples. Aimee named him Harrison Ray after me and Mr. Montgomery. Mariah calls him Harry, and I've already found myself calling him Harry, too."

"Hmm. Right after you were born Dad called you Harry. Until your mother ordered him to stop. Still, a name doesn't make him yours. Or red hair and dimples."

"No. But I have a feeling inside me and it's telling me that Harry is mine," Finn reasoned. "I was right about Sassy being my sister. I'm right about Harry, too."

Orin sighed. "Could be you're letting your wants interfere with your reasoning. These past few years your brothers and sister have been having children. It's only natural for you to want the same."

Finn wiped a weary hand across his forehead and tried not to let his father's suggestion annoy him. It was true his siblings were having babies left and right. But that hardly meant Finn wanted the same for himself. Hell, he didn't even have a steady girlfriend. And rarely found the time to go out on a casual date, much less make room in his life for a wife and child.

Finn said, "Well, don't worry, Dad. Monday morning Mariah and I are taking Harry into town and having a DNA test done."

"Good. Was this the aunt's idea, or yours?"

Finn grimaced. "We both thought it was the best way to resolve the issue."

"Well, apparently she isn't grabbing the first chance to push the baby off on you. Has she or any of her family demanded money yet?"

It wasn't like his father to bring up the issue of money. Especially where a child's welfare was concerned. But this was an unusual circumstance, one that had left Finn feeling a little embarrassed. Having one-night stands wasn't his style. But the revelation of Harry had certainly made him look like an irresponsible lothario. Now his father was probably thinking Finn's philandering was going to cost the family a fortune.

Biting back a groan, he said, "There is no Montgomery family to speak of, Dad. It's just Mariah. And she's hardly out for money." Resting a shoulder against the board fence of the stall, Finn gazed at the back of the ranch house some fifty yards away. When he'd left to come out here to the barns, Mariah had been in the kitchen preparing some sort of dessert she planned to bake. She'd been quiet and reflective, and Finn didn't have to wonder what was on her mind. "I am concerned about her, though. She considers herself Harry's mother. Giving him up is going to crush her."

"She needs to remember she's only the aunt. Whether it's you or some other man, Harry has a father and he has every right to his son."

Finn absently reached over and stroked the stallion's jaw. "It's not just the issue of Harry. Without her dad and sister to train the horses, the ranch is going broke. She's been forced to put it up for sale. If I take Harry she'll be losing him and her home. So I'm not exactly dealing with a pleasant situation up here, Dad."

His father was silent for so long Finn thought the connection between them had broken.

"Dad, are you still there?"

"Yes, son. Just thinking. How old is this woman, anyway?"

Finn mouthed a curse word under his breath. "She's twenty-eight. But what the heck does her age have to do with anything?"

"Finn, you're not up there to fix Ms. Montgomery's problems. This is about a baby and whether you're the father. I hope you remember that."

What did his father think he was? A teenager, whose brain was dictated by raging hormones instead of common sense? The idea clamped his jaw tight.

Finn's silence must have made a point. After a moment, Orin asked, "Are you okay, son? Do you need for me or one of your brothers to come up there?"

His slouched stance suddenly went rigid as he straightened away from the fence. "No! I'll handle this in my own way!"

"There's no need for you to get defensive, Finn."

He was more than defensive. He was disappointed and hurt that his father didn't trust him to use a lick of sense about Harry or Mariah, or any of it.

"Look, Dad, don't expect me to just brush Mariah's feelings aside. Maybe that's the way Gramps would do it. But not me!"

"Okay, Finn. You want to keep your family out of it, so handle it your own way."

It was all Finn could do to keep from yelling out a curse word. "I'm not trying to keep my family out of this. But this is my baby. Not yours or Clancy's or Rafe's or Evan's or Bowie's. I think I have enough sense to decide what my son does or doesn't need!"

"Fine," Orin said bluntly. "So what are your plans? When do you think you'll be coming home?"

"I'll be staying here on Stallion Canyon until we get the results of the DNA test," Finn told him.

"But that could be weeks! I know you haven't forgotten when you and Sassy had the test. It felt like we waited forever on those results."

"I'm hoping the process has speeded up since then," Finn said. "Will you be able to handle my job until I get back? If not, Colley can. He knows as much about horses as I do."

"I can handle it."

His father sounded snippy, but Finn wasn't going to fret about that. The Silver Horn ranch had an endless number of hands and the money to keep everything running in tip-top condition. Moreover, his father had all sorts of family surrounding him and supporting him with whatever endeavor or problem arose.

Mariah had none of those things. Maybe his father could be indifferent to her plight, but Finn couldn't. His feelings had already gotten mixed up with hers. And he didn't have a clue as to how to untangle them. Or whether he even wanted to.

"Thanks, Dad."

"Don't thank me. Just get yourself home—where you belong."

"I'll keep you abreast of things."

Finn ended the connection and jammed the phone back into its leather holder. That was the first time in his adult life that he'd ended a conversation with his father on a tense note, and the realization bothered him. But as much as he loved and respected his father, it was time that Finn stood alone as his own man.

And whether the decisions he made about Harry and Mariah turned out to be right or wrong, or made with his head or his heart, they had to be Finn's own decisions.

Chapter Four

The conversation with his father was still buzzing in his head as Finn walked over to a tall board corral. Inside the enclosure, a group of mares stood dozing beneath a pair of aspen trees. The only mustangs that had ever run over Horn range were the wild ones that just happened to stray onto the ranch's property. When that occurred, the ranch hands were promptly sent out to round up the wild horses and haul them back to their allotted range-land. But if Finn had his own land, he could put as many mustangs on it as he wanted. He could breed and train them without any interference from his family.

Up until now, he'd only dreamed of finding a piece of land in the Carson City area that possessed sustainable grazing and water supply. But now that Harry had come into his life, the idea of becoming more independent had not only germinated; it was rapidly growing.

"I was beginning to think you'd gotten kicked in

the head or something. You've been out here for a long time."

Mariah's voice had Finn turning to see her walking toward him with Harry riding happily in the crook of her arm. A billed cap was on the baby's head to shield his eyes from the late evening sun, while Mariah's red boots had been replaced by a pair of brown ones that were scuffed and scarred with wear.

"Sorry I worried you," he said. "I've been taking my time looking things over." He didn't add that he'd been talking to his father. Sharing the gist of their conversation would only upset her.

When she joined him at the fence, Finn immediately reached for Harry and positioned the boy against his shoulder. Soft baby scents instantly drifted to his nostrils, and the bright, eager gaze in the boy's blue eyes touched something deep inside him. Harry would grow to be a man of the land. Somehow Finn was certain of that. Just as certain as he knew that having a son was going to change the direction of his own life.

Mariah said, "Before Dad died, horses were everywhere. The barns were always freshly painted, the fences erect. Hay and grain would be stacked to the ceiling and there were plenty of ranch hands to deal with the chores. Now it's a ghostly place."

The pensive note he heard in her voice told Finn she wasn't quite as indifferent to her longtime home as she'd first led him to believe.

"It would thrive again," he told her. "In the right hands."

Her sigh was so faint it was barely discernible to his ears. "Maybe the next person can make it successful again. But if I had all the money in the world I wouldn't sink it back into this place."

If one of his brothers spoke in such a negative way about the Silver Horn, Finn would be livid. Passing down the land and legacy was important to every Calhoun family member. If necessary, each one of them would fight with his dying breath to save what their forefathers had worked so hard to build. It was hard to understand Mariah's lack of fight to save her home.

He studied her profile. "I can't decide if you love this place or hate it."

"I don't hate the ranch or the horses. I guess my feelings are mixed," she admitted.

"Considering all that's happened, I'd probably be feeling mixed up, too."

Her head turned toward him and Finn watched the warm wind play with the baby-fine tendrils at her hairline. The black curls were a vivid contrast against her creamy skin, and for a moment Finn wondered how her skin would taste. How would she react if he placed his lips against her temple?

As the erotic questions swirled through his head, Harry's squirms reminded Finn where that sort of thinking had gotten him. The last thing he needed right now was to let his libido lead him down a reckless path with this woman.

"Forgive me if I sound like a bitter, ungrateful person," she said. "I'm not really. It's just that—well, I lost Dad, then Aimee. Then all of a sudden it was just me and little Harry. And everything around me seems to be slipping away."

Finn wanted to reach over and lay a steadying hand on her shoulder. He longed to see her smile and hear her promise she was going to be happy again no matter where her plans took her. But the past seemed to be overwhelming her.

"I'm going to be frank, Mariah. I'm not sure that getting rid of your home is the right answer for you."

Turning her back to him, she rested her forearms on one of the lower rails of the board fence and stared out at the broodmares. There was no grass in the paddock; only a few spindly weeds dotted the dusty ground. Obviously, the mares were getting fed daily, but it wasn't the sort of nutrition they needed to produce sturdy foals. Now was hardly the time for him to point that out to Mariah, though.

No time would be right for that, Finn. This isn't your place, your horses or your woman. Someone else will have to deal with Mariah's problems. Not you.

The sound of her voice suddenly drowned out the one going on in his head.

"Aimee used to talk about Harry growing up and taking over the reins of Stallion Canyon. But if it turns out that he—well, goes with you to Nevada, then this place won't matter. You'll have plenty to pass on to him."

So that was it, Finn thought. Losing Harry was taking away her purpose, her drive to fight for her home.

He gazed down at the baby, who was happily taking in the sights and sounds of the outdoors. Even though he'd only met his son a few hours ago, plans for his future were already building in Finn and taking hold of his heart. How would he feel if the DNA said Harry belonged to some other man? All his dreams would suddenly be snatched away. The way he was going to snatch them away from Mariah if he left with Harry.

Stop being so damned softhearted, Finn. You're the one who's been wronged. If Harry truly is your son, then you've missed seeing him born and lost the first four months of his life. All because this woman and her sister didn't see fit to tell you a baby was coming.

Mentally shaking away the pestering thoughts, he said to Mariah, "Harry will ultimately inherit my share of the Silver Horn. But right now my main objective is to give him a home."

As soon as the remark passed his lips, her head jerked around and she stabbed him with a resentful stare. "Excuse me, but Harry hasn't exactly been homeless."

Seeing he was going to have to be more careful with his words, Finn said, "Sorry. That didn't come out exactly right. I meant a home with me."

"That depends on the DNA test." She turned and motioned toward a connecting barn. "It's time to do the evening feeding. If you'd be kind enough to see after Harry, I'll get to work."

She started walking toward the end of the big white barn and Finn automatically fell into step beside her. "I'd be glad to watch Harry. But I'm curious. What do you normally do with the baby while you tend to your outside chores? Doesn't anyone come around to help you with him?"

"A nanny keeps him during the weekdays while I'm at school. But she leaves in the evenings before feeding time. When he was smaller I put him in his stroller and parked it in a safe spot where I could keep an eye on him. But now that he's grown enough to sit in a propped position, I put him in a little wagon with side boards. He enjoys that even more than the stroller. Especially when I pull him along behind me. Follow me and I'll show you."

Inside a large, dusty feed room filled with sacks and barrels of mixed grain, rubber buckets, galvanized tubs, and scoops, Mariah pulled out a red wagon with wooden side boards. The inside was lined and padded with a thick blanket.

"I made a seat belt for him with the straps from a child's old car seat. And I use this baby pillow to prop in front of him for extra support. It works great," she told Finn. "I don't have to worry about him toppling over or trying to pull himself out. Just sit him here and I'll show you how to buckle him up."

He placed Harry at the back end of the wagon and Mariah clipped the safety straps across the boy's chest. All the while, she was incredibly aware of Finn standing next to her.

These past few hours, her emotions had been on a violent roller coaster. The lonely woman in her was relishing every moment of his rugged presence. But part of her was weeping at the thought of his taking her baby away. Her only hope of hanging on to Harry was to have Finn's DNA be a mismatch. But would that really solve anything? Harry deserved a father. She'd have to keep searching, and the next man might not be daddy material at all.

"Very ingenious," he said with a grin. "You ought to put these things on the market."

Straightening to her full height, she tried her best to smile. "I'd rather just keep the little invention to myself."

She hurriedly moved away and began scooping grain into one of the heavy rubber buckets. One, two, three. She continued counting until she reached six, then started on another bucket.

From the corner of her eye, she could see Finn watching her. What was he thinking? Earlier this afternoon, there'd been odd moments when she'd thought she'd seen masculine appreciation in his eyes, maybe even a hint of attraction. But that could've been her imagination working overtime. After all, it had been so long since she'd had a man look at her in a sexual way that she wasn't sure she would recognize the signs.

"Can I help you measure the feed?" he asked.

"No thanks. I can handle this. Just take Harry on outside so he won't breath in the grain dust."

For a moment she thought he was going to protest, but after a shrug of one shoulder, he grabbed the wagon tongue and pulled Harry out of the feed room. Once he was out of sight, Mariah bent her head and drew in a long, bracing breath. She had to collect herself. The man was going to be around for several more days. She couldn't fall apart every time he came near her.

By the time she carried the feed buckets out of the barn, she noticed Finn had parked the wagon beneath a canyon mahogany so that Harry would be shaded. As soon as he spotted her at the gate to the mares' paddock, he left the baby to join her.

"Harry is perfectly content, so let me help you with one of those," he said, while reaching for one of the buckets.

"Thanks," she told him. "Just pour it into one of those long troughs. I'll fill the other one."

Once the mares were lined up at the trough, the two of them made their way out of the small paddock.

"I hope you're giving the mares adequate hay. Carrying babies, they especially need the nutrition."

Mariah would be the first to admit she didn't know a whole lot about horse care. Not when she compared her equine knowledge to Aimee and her father. Still, it irked her to have this man telling her what she needed to be doing with her own animals.

"I do," she answered. "But I'm not sure how much longer I can keep it up. Hay is expensive. If I don't sell the horses soon I may have to turn them out on the range and let them scavenge for whatever grazing they can find."

He stopped in his tracks and stared at her in disbelief.

"Mariah, no! All five of those mares are near foaling. They need to be monitored closely. If they have trouble—"

"Look, Finn, I realize you mean well. But I can't afford the best hay or grain. I can't even afford a vet. If the mares have trouble foaling the most I can do is call on Ringo to help. Together we'll try our best to get the foals delivered safely."

"Is he a vet?"

Her short laugh was like a mocking snort. "He's a mechanic by trade. He kept Dad's tractors and trucks running. All he knows is to pour out feed, toss hay and make sure the water troughs are full. But he'll do whatever he can to help."

He sighed and stroked his fingers against his jawline as though she'd just thrown him a heavy problem, one that he had no idea how to deal with. Mariah could've told him that she'd been feeling that same heavy burden for months now.

Frowning, she asked, "What's wrong? None of this is your problem. So you needn't concern yourself."

"I'm sorry if it seems like I'm intruding—"

"You are intruding," she interrupted.

"But I'm concerned about the mares."

For as long as Mariah could remember, it had always

been horses first in the Montgomery family. Many times she'd longed to have her father's undivided attention, even for only one day. Now she was seeing the very same thing with this man.

"So am I. But I'm doing the best I can." She glanced over her shoulder to make sure Harry was safe before she continued walking.

Three long strides and he was back at her side. "I'm only trying to help, Mariah."

She heaved out a heavy breath. "Then find me a buyer. Quick."

"For the horses? Or the ranch?" he questioned.

"Both."

"Tell me, Mariah, what if someone came along right this minute and bought you out?" he asked. "Do you have a plan?"

Did he really care or was he just being nosy? she wondered.

"My plan is to be happy," she said. "No matter where I go. Or what I do."

His lips took on a sardonic twist. "Really? I'm not sure you know how."

Later that evening, Mariah cooked a quick meal of salad and spaghetti. Afterward, Finn helped her clean the kitchen and then excused himself to his bedroom to make a phone call.

While Finn was occupied, Mariah gave Harry a bath, then carried him to the nursery where she dressed him in blue pajamas printed with cats and dogs.

"Okay, little guy. Let Mommy brush your red curls and then you'll be all ready for a visit from the sandman." While she hummed a lullaby beneath her breath, she pushed the baby brush through Harry's fine hair until a red curly strip stood up in the middle of his head. "Wow! What a handsome guy you are now!"

Harry cooed and gave her a toothless grin. Laughing at his precious face, Mariah bent her head and pressed kisses to his fat cheeks, which in turn made the baby giggle loudly.

Behind them, Finn knocked lightly on the door facing. "Am I interrupting?" he asked.

He'd interrupted everything, Mariah thought. Especially her peace of mind. For weeks now, she'd been convinced that selling the ranch and starting a new life elsewhere was exactly what she needed and wanted. Now, he had her questioning her own feelings and wondering if she was about to make a giant mistake.

"No. I'm only getting Harry ready for bed. He usually falls asleep around this time in the evenings. Was there something you needed? If your room isn't comfortable, there's another guest room just down the hall."

"As long as I have a place to lay my head, I'm happy," he told her. "This time of the year I spend most nights sleeping on a cot in the foaling barn, anyway. Thankfully, most of the Horn mares have already delivered, and breeding next year's foals has started."

"Sounds like you have lots of babies coming at once. You must be a busy man in the spring."

"It's hectic. One of these mornings I expect to look in the bathroom mirror and see that my hair has turned white. But I love this time of year. New babies—new beginnings. It's exciting."

He walked over to where she had Harry lying atop the small dressing table, and as he stood beside her, she was suddenly remembering the few moments she'd stood with her cheek pressed to his chest. His arms had felt so warm and strong, and the scent of him had filled her senses with erotic thoughts. Just thinking of it now warmed her cheeks and left her feeling horribly foolish. If she'd been the one he'd made love to, if she'd been the one who'd borne his child, things would be so different now, she thought. Because she couldn't imagine loving this man only once. Unlike Aimee, she would've done everything in her power to keep him in her life.

He said, "Actually, I wanted to discuss something with you. Whenever you have a free moment."

She glanced over to see he'd removed his long-sleeved shirt and replaced it with a gray T-shirt. The cotton jersey fabric clung to his broad chest and revealed a pair of heavily muscled arms. The sight rattled her senses so much that she swiftly jerked her gaze back to the safety of Harry's sweet face.

"Uh—let's go to the back porch," she suggested. "It's cooled off nicely and there's a playpen back there for Harry."

"Sounds good."

With Finn carrying the baby, they walked through the house and onto the back porch. The long planked floor stretched the full length of the back of the house and was protected from the weather by a tin roof. At one end several pieces of wicker lawn furniture were grouped together. Behind the chairs, next to the wall of the house, was a small playpen equipped with blankets and a small pillow.

"I'll just hold Harry for a while," he said.

He eased his long frame into one of the chairs and Mariah took the seat opposite from him. As she watched him settle Harry in a comfortable position against his chest, she couldn't help but notice how gentle he was with the baby. It was a reassuring sight. If Finn truly was Harry's father, he'd be a loving one, at least.

"You have a beautiful view out here with the pine trees and the mountains in the distance. How many acres does Stallion Canyon cover?"

"Close to six thousand," she answered.

"You get much rain up here?"

"No. Hardly any in the summer. A little more in the autumn season. Normally we do get a fair amount of snow, though, and that helps. Dad always kept a few of the hay meadows irrigated. But the irrigation system needs repairing. Like everything else around here."

He didn't reply, and she wondered what he was thinking as he stared off toward the western horizon where a purple haze was darkening the skyline. Yes, Stallion Canyon was a beautiful place. Strange that it had taken this man to make her remember just how beautiful.

He said, "I've been doing some thinking this afternoon. About you and Harry."

Something about the quiet tone in his voice made her go on sudden alert. "What about us?"

His gaze returned to her face and Mariah's heart thumped with anticipation. In spite of the serious expression on his face, there was an appealing look in his blue eyes and it melted her like spring snow beneath a warm sun.

"I wanted to ask if you'd be willing to travel to the Silver Horn and stay for a while." He held up a hand before she could reply. "That is, if the DNA proves Harry to be my son," he added.

Without even knowing how she got there, Mariah

was instantly standing on her feet. "To Nevada? With you and Harry?"

He shot her a crooked grin and Mariah's gaze was drawn to his white teeth and the faint dimples bracketing his lips. He was the most masculine man she'd ever encountered, and each time she looked at him the act of breathing grew more difficult. Being around this man for only a few hours had already shaken her. A steady dose of his company would no doubt turn her into a complete fool.

"Yes. With me and Harry and the rest of the family," he said easily. "Harry is accustomed to you. It would be much easier for him to make the transition to a strange place if you were with him. We have plenty of room. And you wouldn't have to lift a finger. Just be there for Harry's needs."

Finn was inviting her to his home in Nevada. The idea staggered her. What normal woman with a beating heart could resist such an opportunity? But he was getting way ahead of himself. And she couldn't let her romantic notions run wild.

Her mouth was suddenly so dry she had to swallow before she could manage to say a word. "Aren't you assuming quite a bit? You can't be certain of what the DNA test is going to say. Before either of us makes plans regarding Harry, we need to see the results."

"We'll waste the time and the money on the DNA test to put your mind at ease. But I can tell you right now— I'm Harry's father."

She couldn't let his confident attitude shake her. "We'll see," she replied. "But in the meantime, I have two more weeks of school. I can't go anywhere."

He looked disappointed and Mariah wondered if his reaction was because of her or Harry.

Don't be ridiculous, Mariah. The man didn't invite you to his home for romantic reasons. He's already convinced that Harry is his son. He's only thinking about the baby's welfare. Not you.

He slanted a thoughtful glance at her. "Well, could be that the results will return about the time you finish your school term. Would you be willing to make the trip then?"

She stared at him in disbelief. Was having her with Harry really that important to him? She couldn't imagine it. Not when he could easily hire a full-time nanny. "I'd have to think about that. I have so many responsibilities here. The ranch, the horses and—"

The remainder of her words trailed away as he suddenly rose from the chair and carried Harry over to the playpen. As he carefully deposited the baby on his back, he said, "Before you say anything else, Mariah, let me get Harry settled."

After pulling a light blanket up to the boy's waist, he offered him a rubber teething ring. Once Harry was happily chewing on the ring and kicking his feet, he left the baby and came to stand next to her. The nearness of his tall, lanky body towering over hers whipped her senses into a wild frenzy.

He said, "Before my invitation, you'd pretty much written this ranch off. Now all of a sudden you can't leave it."

Darkness had settled over the backyard, but there was enough light slanting through the windows of the kitchen to illuminate the porch. She watched in fascination as patches of golden glow and gray shadows played across his rugged features.

"My feelings concerning the ranch have nothing to do with it," she countered. "Other than the little work Ringo does around here, I'm the sole caretaker. I have to be here to keep things going."

"That's no problem. I'll hire someone to take care of the horses and whatever else is needed done around here."

Her heart was suddenly racing at such a frantic pace, she unconsciously pressed her fingers to the middle of her chest. "You'd do that?"

A faint smile brought the dimple back to his cheek. "Of course I would. If Harry goes to the Horn I want him to be happy. Having you with him would surely help him make the transition."

Naturally his concern was all about Harry. But for one moment there, Mariah wanted to believe he was thinking of her. She wanted to think he was extending the invitation so she wouldn't feel so cut off from Harry. Dear God, she was turning into a mushy idiot.

Unable to look him in the eye, she turned her back to him and gulped in a breath of fresh air. She had to get a grip before she fell to pieces right here in front of him. "I see. Well, if you do take Harry—I'm not sure that my going along would be wise. He'd get to thinking I belonged there with him. And eventually I'd have to leave. He wouldn't understand why I was gone."

Her last words were choked and she quickly bent her head in an attempt to conceal the tears that were rushing to her eyes. She didn't want Finn to see a shattered woman. She wanted him to believe that she was strong enough to survive anything. And with or without Harry, she would survive, she forcefully reminded herself. She had no other choice.

Suddenly his hands wrapped around her upper arms and their warmth rushed through her like a fierce wildfire, scorching her senses and melting her resistance.

"You could be right about that, Mariah. I'm only trying to think of a way to make this easier for all three of us."

Agony twisted her insides as she turned back to him. "That's impossible, Finn. Besides, what if you're not the father? Other than Bryce, I wouldn't have a clue who it might be. What would happen to Harry if some stranger laid claim to him? The whole idea makes me shudder with fear."

His eyes narrowed thoughtfully. "Hmm. All this time I believed you didn't want my DNA to match. Now it sounds like you do."

A blush stung her cheeks. "Okay. Maybe I was hoping that...just a little," she admitted. "But this afternoon I've been doing some thinking, too. And I've decided that you—"

When she couldn't find the words to go on, he finished for her. "I'm the lesser of two evils?"

Somehow her face grew even hotter. "Something like that," she mumbled. "I don't know all that much about you yet. But I can see you'd be good to Harry."

"What about Aimee's old boyfriend? Is he the fathering sort?"

"Bryce?" She shook her head. "Not at all. From what Aimee said, he didn't want kids with his first wife. And he didn't want them with Aimee. If he turned out to be the father, God help us."

His hands tightened on her upper arms. "Don't worry.

I'm the father," he murmured. His hands eased their grip on her arms and slid slowly upward until they were resting upon her shoulders. "And if we put our minds together and concentrate on doing everything for Harry's sake, then everything else will take care of itself."

As his last words trailed away with the night breeze, Mariah saw his gaze settle on her lips. After that she wasn't sure if he bent his head first or if she rose up on her toes, but something caused their faces to come together. And then his lips were fastening over hers, his arms pulling her tight against his hard body.

Too dazed to think, Mariah's lips automatically parted beneath his. Her arms slipped up and around his neck, while the front of her body nestled itself against a slab of masculine muscle. It didn't matter if this was all for Harry's sake. All that mattered was that he was making her feel like a woman. A woman who was needed and wanted.

Her senses were spinning faster and faster, until everything was a blur. She couldn't move or think. But she could certainly feel. The search of his hard lips upon hers was tugging her to a dark, sweet place that beckoned her to move closer, to stay in the enchanting web of his arms.

But suddenly his head lifted and a cool wind brushed across her face and touched her heated lips. Gulping in a deep breath, she opened her eyes to see that he was gazing down at her. It was then she noticed that his hands were resting at the base of her throat, where a vein throbbed against his fingers.

"Mariah," he whispered.

He made her name sound like a sexy plea and it was all she could do to keep from groaning aloud.

"Why did you do that?" she asked hoarsely.

A faint smile curved his lips. "I'm a curious man and you're a beautiful woman. A plus B equals C."

"That's not the way algebra works."

He chuckled lowly. "You're right. That's not algebra. That's my own special equation."

He was making light of the whole thing and it would be best if she did, too. But his kiss had shaken her to the very depths of her being. And she was sick of men never taking her seriously, tired of being considered a pleasant pastime and nothing more.

"Very cute," she muttered, then quickly turned away from him and walked over to Harry's playpen. "But I've had enough laughs for one night. I'm putting Harry and myself to bed."

She was bending over to pick up Harry when Finn's hands caught her around the waist and tugged her straight back into his arms.

"If you thought that was for laughs, then maybe I'd better do it over."

Before she could react, he'd already fastened his lips over hers. And this time there was no mistaking the raw hunger in his kiss.

Mariah didn't know how long she stood there in his arms, his lips feasting on hers. She eventually heard herself groaning and then he was stepping away, staring down at her flushed face.

"Sweet dreams, Mariah."

He walked off the porch and into the shadows that stretched toward the barns. Mariah stood there until she'd regained her breath, then collected Harry from the playpen and hurried into the house.

Chapter Five

"Is anything wrong with your eggs? If they don't suit you I can cook more."

Finn looked up from his plate and across the breakfast table to Mariah. With Harry sitting in a high chair next to her, she was offering the baby a spoonful of mushy-looking oatmeal. Harry appeared to be enjoying every bite, even those that were dripping onto his chin.

"The eggs taste fine." To prove it, Finn shoveled up a forkful of the fried eggs he'd covered with green chili sauce. "I was just thinking, that's all."

Thinking, hell. That was hardly what he'd been doing since he kissed Mariah last night. His mind had been whirling like a dust devil. What had possessed him to kiss her, not once, but twice? It wasn't like him to lose his head over a woman he'd just met! At least, not since that brief fling with Aimee. And looking at Harry ought to remind him of the results of that particular instant attraction. Yet this thing he was feeling about Mariah was different. It was more than attraction. She made him forget all common sense.

"If you're thinking about that kiss, then don't," she said stiffly. "I've already forgotten it and you should, too."

"Then why did you bring it up?" he countered.

She frowned as pink color spread across her cheeks and Finn could only think how pretty she looked, even when she was vexed. This morning she was wearing a black button-up blouse with little sleeves that barely covered the ball of her shoulder. Her black hair was tied back from her face with a white silk scarf, but it hardly contained the long waves falling around her shoulders. Her bare skin glowed like a pearl that had been polished between two fingers, while her lips glistened moist and soft. She looked fresh and erotic and oh, so young. And Finn was finding it impossible to keep his eyes off her.

She said, "Because you have a miserable look on your face and I suspect you're regretting you kissed me once. Much less twice."

"I'm not regretting anything," he muttered. And given the chance, he'd do it again. But he wasn't about to let her in on that secret.

"Oh," she said stiffly. "So when you first get up in the mornings, it's normal for you to look like you could commit murder."

Groaning, Finn wiped a hand over his face, then reached for the china cup filled with steaming coffee. "Sorry. I have a lot of things on my mind. And about last night—I don't usually go around kissing women like that. But I—"

"Thought it might be a good tool of persuasion? Or you needed to end the day with a few kicks?"

A sleepless night, added to all that had happened to him yesterday, had left Finn feeling addled this morning, and Mariah's brittle comments were only compounding the sluggishness of his brain.

He sipped the coffee in hopes it would clear the heavy fog behind his eyes, while across the table she used her fork to push the bacon and eggs from one side of her plate to the other.

"Those kisses had nothing to do with Nevada or Harry or fun," he said crossly. "Can't a man be near a woman just for the simple pleasure? Why does there have to be ulterior motives behind a couple of kisses?"

Sighing, she said, "I just don't like being used. That's all."

"Neither do I. So let's forget it," he suggested. "It's a new day. Let's start over. What do you say?"

She looked across the table at him and Finn noticed her gray eyes were full of lost, lonely shadows. The sight made him feel like a heel. It made him want to cradle her in his arms and tell her she was special. That he would never intentionally hurt or use her.

A tentative smile tugged at the corners of her mouth. "That's a good idea. So, tell me, now that you've slept on it, are you still planning on staying until we get the test results?"

She was giving him a crack to wriggle through. If Finn was ever going to change his mind about being in this woman's company for the next several days, he needed to do it now. But Harry was too important and he wasn't going to leave this ranch without him.

He reached for the thermal pot sitting in the middle

of the table. As he warmed his coffee, he said, "I'm staying."

Her fork paused in midair. "Oh. Did you bring enough things with you for a lengthy stay? I mean, like extra clothes and that sort of stuff."

Cradling his coffee cup with both hands, he leaned back in his chair. "Enough. But I think I'll drive into town this morning and pick up a few more things I could use while I'm here. If you and Harry need anything, make a list and I'll pick it up for you. Or better yet, you're welcome to come with me."

She shook her head. "Thanks, but I have too much to do here in the house before I go back to work in the morning."

"I'm sure Harry can always use formula and diapers," he pointed out. "Let me know what kind and I'll pick some up."

She looked like she wanted to argue, and Finn decided she was reluctant to relinquish any part of Harry's care to him. Which was only natural, he supposed. But how long was it going to take before she finally let go of the baby? When the DNA made it clear Finn was the father? Or did she ever plan to let go?

"Okay. I'll make a list," she said.

"Good."

Finn ate the remaining bacon and eggs on his plate, then drained his coffee cup. By the time he was finished, Mariah had already risen from her chair and started gathering dirty dishes from the tabletop.

"I need to get to the barn and start feeding," she said. "I'd be grateful if you could watch Harry. It would save me bundling him up and taking him out with me. It's rather cool this morning."

Finn left the table and carried his dirty dishes over to the sink. "You stay in and watch Harry. I'll tend to the feeding."

She walked over to him. "I know I mentioned you helping out around here. But I don't expect you to do my chores."

"Look, Mariah, I'm not used to being idle. Besides, caring for horses is a pleasure for me." He walked over to the bar, where he'd left his hat. As he levered the brim over his forehead, he said, "By the way, if you're still in a hurry to get rid of the mustangs, I think I can come up with a new home for them."

Her eyes narrowed with speculation. "A new home? Where?"

"I need to make a few phone calls before I say more. We'll talk about it later." On his way out of the kitchen, he paused at Harry's high chair and squatted down to the baby's level. Emotions swelled in his chest as he touched a forefinger to the dimple in Harry's cheek. "That grin of yours is going to melt all the girls' hearts."

As though he understood, Harry kicked both legs and squealed. Across the way, Mariah laughed softly and the warm sound had him looking over to see a tender smile on her face. The expression made her features even lovelier.

"I think Harry has already melted a few hearts," she said. "Including yours."

Straddling a river, the little town of Alturas sat in a valley with a ridge of tall mountains to the east, forest to the north and flat wetlands to the south. A wide main street was lined on either side by quaint shops and businesses, some housed in buildings that had been around for a century or more. As Finn negotiated his truck through the sparse Sunday traffic, it dawned on him that this community had been Mariah's life for the past twenty years.

Would she still continue to live here once he took Harry home to the Silver Horn?

Why wouldn't she? Her teaching job is here. Her friends and acquaintances. Once the ranch sells, she'll probably move to a little rental here in town. And eventually, she'll find a man to marry. She'll raise children, not horses. And after a while, you and Stallion Canyon will be nothing more than a dim memory to her.

The voice going off in Finn's head continued to nag at him, even after he finished his shopping and stopped at a little diner on the edge of town. After having a slice of pie and a cup of coffee, he climbed back in his truck, but made no move to start the engine. Instead, he pulled out his cell phone and punched the number to his oldest brother. According to his watch, it would be another hour and a half before his brother and family left for church.

After the third ring, Clancy's voice boomed in Finn's ear.

"Hey, Finn! How's it going? Dad told us you've seen the baby. What's he like?"

The mention of Harry sent a spurt of joy through Finn. "He has red in his hair and dimples in his cheeks. And he's a happy little guy. You'll fall in love with him."

"Sounds like you already have."

"Yeah. I guess I have," he admitted.

Clancy said, "I might as well tell you that Dad's concerned about you. He says when you two talked yesterday you didn't sound like yourself."

"That's because I was disagreeing with him," Finn

said. "He's not a bit happy about me staying up here until the DNA results get back."

"Oh. He didn't mention that. But I could tell he was steamed about something. So this means you'll probably be up there two or three weeks?"

Pushing the brim of his hat to the back of his head, Finn wiped a hand across his forehead. "Something like that. I don't want to leave without the baby, Clancy. I'm already convinced he's mine. But Mariah, that's Harry's aunt, wants proof."

Clancy's reaction was a heavy sigh.

"What's the matter?" Finn asked. "You think I'm being selfish for taking that much time off from my job?"

"No," Clancy was quick to reply. "If anyone on the ranch deserves time off, it's you, Finn. Dear Lord, you and Rafe both put in far more hours than any one man should. I just don't want you to have any trouble with this woman. I mean, where the baby is concerned."

Finn could've told Clancy that he was already having trouble with Mariah. But the problem had nothing to do with Harry. It was all about Finn keeping his hands off the woman.

Finn said, "Once the DNA comes back, I don't think she'll give me any problem."

"I'm glad to hear it. And Finn, don't worry. Now that Dad is in full swing again, he can handle the horse division until you get back home."

For several years after their mother had lost her life to a tragic fall, their father, Orin, had retreated into a private shell. Instead of riding the ranch and overseeing the care of the livestock, he'd rarely emerged from the house. But thankfully that had changed when a daughter he hadn't known about had suddenly walked into his life.

Sassy had renewed their father's zest for living. These days he was back to being a rough-and-ready cowboy and had acquired a girlfriend to boot.

Finn rubbed fingers against the furrows in his brow. "There's something else, Clancy. Mariah has ten mustangs. A stallion, four geldings and five broodmares, all of which are soon to foal. I haven't told her yet, but I'm going to buy them."

He expected to hear a gasp out of Clancy. Instead, silence stretched on and on.

"Clancy? Did you hear me?"

"Yeah. Sorry. I don't know what to say. Except that you're asking for trouble. Dad and Gramps aren't going to bend."

Finn muttered a curse under his breath. "Don't worry, I'll find a home for them—as far away from the Horn as I can find."

"Finn, are these horses something you want? Or are you doing this to help Harry's aunt?"

His jaw clamped down even harder. "I'm thirty-two years old, Clancy. Not fifteen. Since when do I have to explain my motives about horses or women or anything else to you?"

"You don't," Clancy quipped. "And what the hell is the matter with you, anyway? Becoming a father normally doesn't turn a man into a smart-ass."

Finn bit back the tart retort on his tongue and sucked in a deep, calming breath. "Okay, so I'm being a jerk. I'm sorry. I—thought you'd understand about the horses. Instead you sound like Dad."

"I just don't want you making any impulsive decisions. The baby should be enough on your plate right now without bringing a bunch of mustangs into the picture."

"Harry and the mustangs go together."

"What does that mean?"

Finn turned the key in the ignition and the truck's engine sprang to life. "I can't explain it now, Clancy. I gotta go."

"Okay. And Finn, I honestly want everything to work out for you. Call me if you need me."

"All I need is for you to trust me, Clancy."

More than a half hour later, back on Stallion Canyon, Mariah stood on the front porch with Harry propped on her hip. After ten minutes, the baby's weight was getting heavy and she desperately wanted to take a seat in one of the wicker armchairs positioned behind her. But she was afraid the man standing on the steps would take it as a sign to join her and she'd already had more of his company than she could stand.

Presently, the stocky, dark-haired man somewhere in his midthirties was gazing out at the western range. Without much spring rain, the grass was sparse, but a bevy of tiny wildflowers had bloomed across the meadow. For some reason she didn't like this man eyeing the ranch as though it was already his. Yet if he was a potential buyer, she needed to remain cordial.

"This is a mighty pretty place, Miss Montgomery," he said. "A man could do a lot with this property."

"A woman could do a lot with it, too," she replied. "If she had enough financial backing to do it with."

He looked back at her. "Does that mean you'd like to keep the place?" A knowing grin narrowed the corners of his eyes. "You know, with the right man and woman working together—"

The sound of an approaching vehicle halted his words and Mariah looked around to see Finn's truck rolling to a stop in the driveway. Thank God he was finally home, she thought with a rush of relief. But what was he doing with hay stacked higher than the cab?

"Is that someone you know?"

"Pardon me," she told him, then shifting Harry to a comfortable position against her shoulder, she walked past the man and out to the front yard gate.

As Finn joined her, he darted a suspicious glance at the man standing on the steps. "Is anything wrong?" he asked.

"Not exactly."

"Then he's company?"

Leaning her head closer to Finn's, she lowered her voice. "I've never met him before. He says he drove out here to talk to me about buying the ranch."

His blue gaze connected with hers, and in that moment Mariah was shocked at how familiar it felt to be near him like this and how dear his features had already become to her.

"You told me you've listed the property with a real estate agent," he said with a frown. "If that's the case, he should be dealing with that person. Not you."

With a hand at her back, he urged her toward the house. "Come on. I'll deal with this."

When they reached the steps, Mariah remained close by Finn's side as she quickly introduced the two men. "Mr. Oakley says he lives down in Likely," she informed Finn. "That's a little town south of here."

The stranger directed an appreciative grin at Mariah

and she instinctively cuddled closer to Finn's side. From the moment the strange man had arrived, he'd been leering at her to the point where she'd begun to doubt whether he was actually here about seeing the ranch. Yet if he was truly a potential buyer, she was hardly in a financial position to send him packing just because he was giving off creepy vibes.

"That's right," the man said. "I work on a little spread down there. But I heard this place was on the market. And from what I can see it's a dandy. A man could do well for himself here."

Finn's lips tightened to a thin line. "Mr. Oakley, I assume you know how to use a telephone?"

The man looked at Finn with comical confusion. "Yeah." He patted a leather pouch attached to his belt. "I've got a cell phone right here."

"Then why didn't you use it before you drove up here?"

Oakley looked as if he'd just been boxed on both jaws. "I—beg your pardon?"

Finn said, "If your interest is in buying this ranch, then you need to be talking with the real estate agent. Not bothering Miss Montgomery by showing up here out of the blue on a Sunday morning."

Stunned that Finn was giving the man such a stinging lecture, Mariah's gaze swapped back and forth between the two men. Oakley's face was beet red, while Finn's features appeared to be chiseled from concrete. What had come over Finn? She'd wanted him to deal with the pushy stranger, but she'd expected him to do it in a polite manner.

"For your information, I did call the agency," Oakley said. "I didn't get an answer."

"Then you should've kept calling until you did get an answer," Finn retorted.

The stranger's eyes narrowed as he stared at Finn. "Who are you, anyway?" he asked curtly. "I thought Miss Montgomery owned this ranch."

Next to her, Mariah could feel Finn go tense and then suddenly his arm was wrapping possessively around her shoulders.

"I am this baby's father. That's who I am," Finn said tersely. "And if I were you, I'd get out of here right now. I don't want to see you around here again. Ever."

Without a word, Oakley stomped off the steps and skirted his way past Finn and Mariah.

Leaving her side, Finn followed a few steps behind the man, then waited at the yard gate until he'd climbed into his truck and driven away. Before the dust from the tires drifted off to the southeast, Mariah carried Harry into the house and placed him in a small playpen she'd erected in the kitchen. Once the baby was settled, she walked back out to the porch to find Finn climbing the steps.

"What was that about?" she asked.

He stepped onto the porch. "Just giving the man the send-off he deserved. He was up to no good and I didn't see any point in playing nice."

"Up to no good?" She shook her head. "Maybe he was a little flirtatious, but that had nothing to do with him being a potential buyer for this ranch. Now you've scared him off!"

He shot her a disgusted look. "Are you kidding me? Would you honestly want a creep like him to own this place? A home you've lived in for twenty years?"

"That's not the point!"

With little more than an inch standing between them, he stared down at her, and Mariah felt her insides begin to tremble. Not with anger, but with raw desire. And the uncontrollable attraction she had toward the cowboy aggravated her as much as his authoritative attitude.

"You're telling me it doesn't matter who winds up here?" he demanded. "Just as long as you have the money?"

"You make it all sound nasty!" she shot back at him. "And you're doing that to make me forget about your— rude behavior!"

"Maybe you'd better explain that," he said tightly.

"Yes, Oakley was a creep. But you could've gotten rid of him in a nicer way."

"Nice, hell! If you think a man like him understands nice, then you're too damned naive to be living out here alone!"

Furious now, she said, "You don't own this ranch. And you certainly don't own me. From now on I'll handle my personal business."

His nostrils flared and though the sparks in his eyes were fueled by anger, the sight of them made her wonder if he made love with the same sort of unleashed passion. The notion sent a shiver of excitement slithering down her spine.

"You think— Oh, to hell with it," he muttered.

He turned to leave the porch and Mariah instantly snatched hold of his forearm.

"Finn, I'm trying to understand your behavior," she said, her voice growing softer with each word. "But you're not making it easy."

He turned back to her and Mariah's heart lurched into a wild gallop as his hands closed over her shoulders.

"Then I need to make things plainer, Mariah. Maybe

I ran that creep off because I don't want him, or any man, thinking they have a snowball's chance in hell of doing this."

This? The question had barely had time to zing through her thoughts when she saw his head lowering to hers. Yet the realization that he was about to kiss her wasn't enough to make her step back. If anything, she wanted to step into him. She wanted to feel his arms around her once again, to experience the taste of his hard, searching lips.

In a feeble attempt at resistance, she planted her palms against his chest, but before she could push a measurable distance between them, the warmth of his muscles seeped into her hands and raced up her arms. The sensation was so pleasurable, she couldn't move, much less make her lungs work in a normal fashion.

"This shouldn't be happening again."

The breathless words rushed past her parted lips but did little to slow the downward descent of his head.

"Probably not," he whispered, his mouth touching hers ever so softly. "But I don't think either of us is going to stop it."

Chapter Six

Mariah had never been kissed outside in broad daylight, not like this. It made her feel exposed and naked and even a bit wicked. Finn's lips were making a hungry foray over hers, turning her into a melted mess, making it impossible for her to think.

Closer. That was the only thing she wanted, needed. With that one thing on her mind, her hands instinctively moved to the back of his neck, the front of her body arched into his, while their lips rocked back and forth to a rhythm only they could hear.

Her head began to whirl until she was certain she was floating off into the blue sky. Her breathing stopped and her heart pounded. If the kiss ended, she'd surely die, she thought. But eventually it did end when Finn finally lifted his head.

Sanity rushed into Mariah's brain and with it came the reality of how lost she'd become in Finn's embrace.

Her fingers were tangled in the hair at the back of his neck, while his hands were splayed against her back, holding her upper body tightly against his.

Through a foggy haze, she stared up at him. "Finn," she whispered hoarsely, "I don't know what's happening to me. To us!"

Not waiting to hear what, if anything, he had to say, she pulled away from him and hurried to the other side of the porch. With her back to him, she stared out at the distant mountains and tried to gain control of her labored breathing. She was trembling all over and her body felt as though a wildfire had ignited inside her and was now spreading from her head to her feet.

The sound of his boots moving across the porch floor alerted her to his approach. Even so, she wasn't ready for the contact of his hand as it rested gently against the back of her shoulder. Until she'd met Finn, she'd had no idea that the simple touch of a man's hand could have the power to shake her like an earthquake.

"Mariah, if it makes you feel any better I'm just as confused as you are. I didn't come here looking to start up a relationship with you."

She swallowed to ease the aching tightness in her throat. "I'm sure you didn't. So what—"

"Am I doing?" he finished for her. "The only thing that's clear to me is when I'm near you I lose control. And I think it happens to you, too."

She turned to face him and her heart was suddenly crying for her to step into his arms, to confess how much the warmth of his embrace chased away her loneliness. But that would be inviting trouble. The sort she didn't need at this point in her life. She had very little experience with men. Especially one as rugged and sexy as

Finn. Hot, brief flings were his style. Not waking up in the same bed with the same woman for the rest of his life.

"Yes. It—" Glad he couldn't see her face, she closed her eyes and licked her swollen lips. "I'm not going to deny that I'm attracted to you. That would be pretty pathetic, wouldn't it? When I just kissed you like—well, like I wanted you."

His fingers tightened on her shoulder and for some inexplicable reason Mariah felt the urge to cry. To brace herself, she bit down hard on her lip and drew in a deep, cleansing breath.

"I want you, too, Mariah."

Such sweet, simple words. But his wanting wasn't the same as hers. She wanted him for more than just a day or night. And she wanted more than just his physical touch. She wanted even the simplest form of his company. To see his smile, hear his voice, watch the ever-changing moods in his sky-blue eyes.

A few years ago, during her college days, she'd thought she felt these things for Kris. But now she realized how lukewarm her feelings for him had been compared to the intensity of her reactions to Finn. And what did it all mean? That she was falling in love with a man she'd met less than twenty-four hours ago? No. Dear heaven, no. His life was back in Nevada on that rich ranch. He'd never think of her in a long-term way.

Bracing herself, she turned and faced him. "It's nothing more than chemistry, and we need to deal with it in an adult way."

"Speak for yourself. I pretty much feel like an adult right now."

She groaned with frustration. "Yesterday we were total strangers, Finn!"

A slow grin spread across his face and Mariah's gaze went straight to his lips. Even now, she wanted to forget the right or wrong of it and tilt her mouth back up to his. Oh my, she had to get a grip and fast.

"If you ask me, a kiss is a pretty good way for us to get to know each other."

She stepped around him before she was tempted to give in to the urge of touching him again. "You need to understand that I'm nothing like Aimee!"

"What the hell does that mean?" he barked.

She started toward the door. "It means I won't go to bed with you just because it would feel good!"

"Thanks for the warning," he flung at her, then stomped off the porch.

Mariah didn't wait to see where he was going. With her eyes full of tears, she hurried into the house.

A few minutes later at the barn, Finn backed his truck up to the door of the feed room and began to unload sacks of grain and alfalfa bales from the bed. As he stacked the feed and hay neatly to one side of the room, Mariah's parting words continued to eat at him.

Damn it, did she think all he wanted from a woman was to get her into bed? Having a brief fling with Aimee didn't make him a playboy. But apparently in Mariah's eyes it did. And after the way he'd been grabbing her up and kissing her, he could hardly blame her for thinking that way.

Using his knee to shove the last bale into place, Finn stepped back from the stacked hay and pulled a bandanna from the back pocket of his jeans. As he wiped the sweat from his face, words of warning from his father and brother swirled through his mind, adding to his frustration.

Deep down, he realized his family was right. Now more than ever, he needed to use common sense. He couldn't let a pair of soulful gray eyes and warm lips turn him into a randy fool.

"What is all of this?"

At the sound of Mariah's voice he quickly glanced over his shoulder to see her standing in the doorway of the feed room. After stomping off the porch in a huff not more than twenty minutes ago, he certainly hadn't expected her to show up here at the barn.

"Where's Harry?" he blurted the question.

"He just went to sleep. He's safe in his crib and I only intend to be here for a few minutes."

"What's the matter? You didn't jab enough barbs in me a while ago? You decided to come out here to the barn and try to cut me a few more times?"

Her lips tightened. "I didn't walk out here to the barn to discuss that—that kissing episode on the porch. We've said enough about it. I came out here because I saw your truck was loaded with hay. And I didn't ask for it."

Relieved that she wasn't going to keep harping about that kiss, or whatever the hell it had been, he turned and walked over to the open doorway. "That's right. You didn't ask for it. I took it upon myself to buy some things for the horses."

The look of disapproval on her face changed to one of concern. Her mouth opened, then after a moment's pause, snapped shut. When it opened a second time he expected to hear a loud protest. Instead, she simply said, "All right. Give me the bill and I'll write you a check."

"That won't be necessary," he told her.

Her shoulders straightened to a stiff line. "It's necessary to me."

He shook his head, while wondering how one moment he could be so on fire to make love to her and the next he wanted to yell with frustration. "We need to talk," he said.

"There's nothing you can say about this—"

"It's not about the hay or the feed." He stepped out of the barn and shut the door behind him. "Let's go to the house. I'll meet you there as soon as I move my truck."

"I'll be in the kitchen," she told him.

A few minutes later, Finn entered the kitchen carrying several packages. As he placed them on the breakfast bar, Mariah left the cabinet counter where she'd been peeling apples and joined him.

He gestured toward the sacks. "I got all the things you had on the list and a few more. There's a little something for you, too," he added sheepishly.

She cast him a guarded glance. "Me? I didn't write anything on the list for myself."

Reaching for the sack closest to her, she pulled out diapers, formula, tiny T-shirts, matching shorts and two pairs of jeans that snapped on the inside of each leg. She couldn't imagine this man strolling through the baby department, picking out clothes for Harry. It only gave her further proof that he wasn't about to shy away from fatherhood.

As she thoughtfully smoothed a finger over the blue fabric, he said, "He might already have plenty of clothes. But I thought they were cute."

"Very cute," she agreed. "I'm surprised you didn't find a Western shirt to go with the jeans."

"I would have, but the store where I bought that stuff didn't have any. And with it being Sunday the Western store was closed," he said. "But give me time and I'll have a stack of shirts for him. And when his feet get big enough, he'll get a pair of boots. Just like mine."

Clearly, Finn was already becoming very attached to Harry. He truly believed he was the father. If his DNA wasn't a match to Harry's, it would crush him. And strangely, Mariah didn't want Finn to go through that heartbreak. Even though it meant he'd be taking the baby to Nevada.

She glanced down at Finn's snub-toed brown boots. To her they looked like they were made from expensive alligator hide. And they probably were. She couldn't imagine him wearing anything fake.

"Considering the size of your foot, that might take a while."

He grinned and Mariah was relieved that the angry tension between them was easing.

"They do make baby-sized boots, you know."

"Yes. And I have no doubt you'll find a pair." She reached for the second sack and removed a little stuffed horse, a bright green teething ring, and lastly, a shiny gold box tied with a pale pink ribbon. The fact that he'd bought her a little gift made her feel awful for losing her temper with him.

"Is this mine?"

"Yes. And don't worry," he told her. "It won't explode or jump out at you."

She pulled the ribbon loose and lifted the lid to see a necklace lying on a bed of velvet. The tiny silver cross attached to a delicate chain was so touching and unexpected she couldn't utter a word.

After a weighty stretch of silence, he said, "It's nothing fancy. But it's real silver. And I thought it suited you."

She swallowed hard. "It's lovely," she murmured. "But you shouldn't have gotten me anything. What you paid for this would've bought a week's work of groceries."

Tangled emotions stirred inside Finn as reached for the necklace. "A woman shouldn't always be practical," he said huskily. "Let me put it on for you."

Expecting her to argue, he was somewhat surprised when she lifted her long hair off her neck and presented her back to him.

Moving closer, Finn positioned the little cross in the hollow of her throat. With the scent of her hair filling his nostrils and her soft skin beckoning every male cell in his body, the temptation to drop his head and press kisses to the back of her bared neck was so strong it caused his hands to tremble.

"Sorry," he murmured as he fumbled with the delicate clasp. "I'm not very practiced at this sort of thing."

"Neither am I," she said softly.

The poignant note in her voice caused his fingers to pause against the nape of her neck. One minute she was all fire and the next as soft as a kitten. And either way, he wanted her. It was that simple, Finn thought.

"You're a beautiful woman, Mariah," he said huskily. "I'm sure other men have given you jewelry before."

She was quiet for long moments and then she turned and smiled wanly up at him. "My dad gave me a bracelet for Christmas one year. And once in grade school, a boy gave me a ring that he'd gotten out of a crank machine.

That little piece of plastic turned out to be much more heartfelt than a diamond I received...well, later on."

A diamond? So she had been deeply involved with a man at one time, he thought. Like a match striking against stone, jealousy flared inside him. He didn't want to think of Mariah loving another man so much that she'd wanted to marry him.

"You were engaged?"

Her head bent downward to hide her face. "For a brief time—a few years ago. It means nothing now."

"If you were wearing his ring it must have meant something back then," he ventured to say.

"I thought it did. But later I realized I was confused about him...and myself."

"Well, that happens," he told her. "I was confused once, too."

She looked up at him and Finn noticed how her fingers were clasping the silver cross as though it were a lifeline.

"You've been engaged before?" she asked.

He grimaced at the memory of Janelle. She'd been a big part of his young life and for a long time he'd expected her to be a part of his future. But she'd had other ideas. Losing her had forced him to grow up. It had also made Finn decide he wanted no part of marriage until he was certain he could deal with the intricacies of a woman's emotional needs.

"Not exactly engaged," he admitted. "We were a steady couple for a long time in high school. It ended before I asked her to marry me."

Curiosity flickered in her gray eyes. "Were you planning to ask her?"

He shrugged while remembering the humiliation he'd

felt when Janelle had turned away from him to marry an older man. "Yes. But at a later time. You see, I was only nineteen. I wasn't ready."

"Oh. Yes, things do get confusing at that age." Turning her head to one side, she licked her lips. "Well, thank you, Finn. It was very thoughtful of you to remember me with a gift."

His gaze took in the strands of black hair resting against the pale creamy skin of her cheek, the silver-gray depths of her eyes and the moist pink curve of her lips. Something about her made his body ache to make love to her, yet at the same time his heart yearned to keep her safe and protected. The conflicting feelings inside him were seesawing back and forth, refusing to settle on common ground.

"The necklace is just a small token—for being such a good mother to Harry. I truly appreciate what you've done for him, Mariah."

Her gaze drifted over to the stuffed horse he'd purchased and he watched a melancholy expression creep over her features.

"It's been a labor of love, Finn."

An uncomfortable lump collected in his throat. He tried to clear it away as he turned and took a seat on one of the bar stools. "Uh—what I wanted to talk to you about, Mariah—there's a reason I don't want any money for the feed and hay. And it has nothing to do with charity. I want to purchase the horses from you."

The look on her face turned to one of disbelief. "The horses? All of them?"

He nodded. "The stallion, the geldings and the mares. Just shoot me a fair price and I'll write you a check. With one stipulation, that is. That I don't have to ship them out immediately. I'd like for them to stay here until the test comes back and we—uh, get everything settled about Harry. By then I'll have found a place to put them. Besides, from the looks of the mares, they're all getting close to foaling. It would be much safer for them to deliver before they have to travel."

Her thoughtful gaze roamed his face. "You're not going to haggle over the price?"

Finn shook his head. "I trust you to be fair."

Easing onto the stool next to his, she stared at the floor. "This past month I've prayed for a buyer to show up. Now you've come along and answered my prayers. But I don't feel good about it." Her head swung back and forth. "Doesn't make much sense, does it? I should be happy. But I—"

"Feel like you're turning loose a part of yourself. I understand."

Thrusting a hand through her hair, she looked at him. "How did you know I felt that way? I didn't even know it myself until this moment."

The torn look in her eyes bothered him far more than it should have. "I know how I'd feel to be giving up a part of my home—what this place had been built on. I figured it would be the same for you. If it will make you feel any better, I can assure you I'll give the horses the best of care."

"I have no concerns about that." Biting down on her bottom lip, her gaze turned away from his. "All right. I'll sell the horses to you. Just give me a bit of time to think over the price. In the meantime, I'm curious about one thing, though."

"What's that?"

She looked at him. "You said you'd have to find a

place to put them. I don't get it. You live on a huge ranch. Surely you have space for ten more horses."

Avoiding her gaze, Finn rubbed the heels of his palms against his thighs. "Not these horses—they're mustangs. My father and grandfather refuse to have any wild horses on the ranch."

Totally surprised, she said, "Oh. I thought you'd have a say in things on the Silver Horn? I mean where the horses are concerned?"

He frowned. "I manage the horse division of the ranch. I oversee the breeding, foaling, training and care of all the equines on the ranch. That includes show horses and working horses."

"Well, clearly they believe you know your job. I don't understand."

He didn't understand it, either, Finn thought grimly. After all these years, he wanted to think his father and grandfather respected his ideas and plans. Instead, they refused to consider them. "The Silver Horn has its own foundation breeding. The same bloodlines have continued on for a hundred years or more. Dad and Gramps don't want it tampered with. You see, they're all about tried-and-true tradition."

"But you could keep the mustangs in a separate area," Mariah argued. "If the ranch covers thousands of acres, what could they possibly hurt?"

"The Silver Horn image."

She mulled that over, then finally replied, "Your folks must be snobs."

"Only where horses and cattle are concerned." The notion had him grunting with wry amusement and then he cast her a meaningful glance. "If I didn't know better, Mariah, you sound like you're proud of those mustangs."

"Well, they were my father and sister's dream. And though there've been plenty of times in my life that I wish I'd never seen a horse, I guess a part of me is proud that Stallion Canyon was founded on mustangs. But I can't keep hanging on to them," she said huskily. "It's not possible. Much less practical."

"And you must be practical."

She left the bar stool and returned to the cabinet. As she sliced an apple into a plastic bowl, she said, "Dad and Aimee were always dreamers. I was always the one who worried over the ranch's finances. And I'm still worrying over them. A person with money has the luxury of being sentimental rather than sensible. I'm not in the position you are, Finn. I have to think about surviving."

So she'd never been the happy-go-lucky sort. Was that the reason her engagement had ended? Finn wondered. Because she'd been all business and no fun?

Hell, Finn. It doesn't matter why or how her engagement ended. That part of her past has nothing to do with you. She loved a man once and he wasn't you. So what? You're not looking for love or marriage.

The need to comfort her suddenly pushed away the irritating voice in his head and he walked over to where she stood and rested his hip against the cabinet. "Mariah, money doesn't fix everything. It doesn't stop you from losing loved ones. Wealthy people get hurt and betrayed. They also get sick and lonely and lost. Just like poor folks do."

She closed her eyes and it was all Finn could do to keep from bending his head and placing his lips on hers. Kissing her stirred more than libido, he realized. It made him dream and want and wish for things that, up until now, he'd never considered important. And he wasn't quite sure if that was a good thing or bad.

"I don't expect selling the horses and the ranch to feel good. But I have to climb out of this hole some way." She opened her eyes and attempted to smile. "Now if you'll excuse me, I'd better go check on Harry."

He didn't want her to go. He wanted to pull her into his arms, stroke her hair and whisper words of reassurance in her ear. He wanted to feel her body go soft and yielding against his, to know that she trusted him completely. But she didn't trust him. He wasn't sure she trusted anybody.

And as he watched her scurry out of the room, Finn decided she was like a little wounded bird, determined to fly away from the very person who wanted to help her.

Chapter Seven

Bright and early the next morning, Mariah and Finn left the ranch to take Harry to the health department in town. After a qualified nurse took swabs from both Finn's and the baby's mouths, she managed to get to school just in time to start the second-hour class, while Finn took Harry back to the ranch, where Linda was waiting to take over her usual role as nanny.

Now a few hours later, Mariah was sitting in a small staff lounge with her friend and fellow teacher, Sage Newcastle, as the two women enjoyed the last few minutes of their lunch break.

"You're actually going to Nevada with this man?" Sage asked in a shocked voice. "I don't believe it!"

Mariah looked over at the blonde thirty-one-year-old divorcée, who'd given up on marriage but not romance.

"Shh! I said I'm considering it. But I don't want the whole staff to know about it!" When Aimee had become a single mother, Mariah had been forced to deal with all sorts of gossip. The rumor mill would surely run rampant if any of the school staff learned she was going to make a trip with Harry's father.

"Besides," she went on, "we only took Harry to the health department this morning to get the DNA swabs sent off. And until I learn that Finn is the father I don't plan on going anywhere with him."

Sage glanced at her with concern. "Having that Nevada cowboy in the house must be causing you a lot of extra work. You look exhausted."

Mariah had to bite her lip to keep from groaning. No way did she want Sage to know she'd lost sleep the past two nights because her mind was fixated on Finn. The way he smelled. The way he looked. The sound of his voice, his laughter. And then there were his kisses. She'd relived them over and over in her mind, as though she'd never been kissed before.

That's because you hadn't been really kissed, Mariah. Not until Finn took you into his arms and like a starving man, made a meal of your lips. Now you're besotted with the way he touched you. The way he made you drunk with desire.

"Yoo-hoo, Mariah! Are you with me?"

Shaking away the mimicking voice in her head, Mariah focused on her friend's earlier remark. "Finn isn't causing extra work. It's—well, everything is going to be in limbo until the DNA comes back."

Sage reached over and placed a comforting hand on Mariah's forearm. "I'm not sure I would've had the courage to call Mr. Calhoun and tell him about Harry. I'm afraid I would've kept the baby all to myself."

"My conscience wouldn't let me do that," she said ruefully. "Harry deserves to have a father."

"Will this Finn make a good one, you think?"

Sage's question caused images of Finn and Harry to flash in the forefront of her mind. She couldn't deny that Harry had already bonded with Finn. And Finn handled the baby as though he were the most special thing on earth. "Finn will make an excellent father. I have no doubts about that."

She didn't add that Finn was a wealthy man and would be able to give Harry every wonderful opportunity in life. That part of the puzzle hardly seemed important now. As he'd told her last evening: money didn't equal happiness. And she figured if Finn didn't have a dime, he'd still have a grin on his face.

Sage said, "Well, that's a relief. Uh—you haven't really told me much about the man. Does he look anything like Harry?"

Mariah shrugged. "Actually, the more I look at the two of them together, the more similarities I see."

"Hmm. Then he must be handsome. Because Harry is adorable," Sage said. "You know, the more I think about it, the more I think you should have me over for dinner one evening. Before Finn goes back to Nevada."

Mariah rose from the long couch where the two women had been sitting and gathered up a stack of books and papers from the corner of a nearby table.

Deliberately changing the subject, she said, "It's almost time for the bell to ring."

"I'm right behind you," Sage told her.

They left the lounge and started down a wide corridor of the high school building. Teenagers were already scurrying past them, while others were opening and closing lockers lined along the walls.

In spite of the stress that went along with teaching young people, Mariah loved her job. To her, the idea of helping a child develop into a productive adult made up for the long hours and minimal salary. The school was her second home and without it these past few months, she would've been truly lost.

"You know," Sage said wryly, "I don't think you want me to meet Harry's dad. That tells me he's either really an ogre, or a dreamboat you want to keep to yourself."

Mariah's chuckle held little humor. "He's a cowboy, Sage. Not your type at all."

Sage's grin was a bit naughty. "I'll bet he's your type, though. You—" She broke off as her gaze zeroed in on the silver cross dangling in the hollow of Mariah's throat. "Oh, how pretty! It looks like a piece from that famous silver designer. Is it?"

Surely not, Mariah thought. Finn wouldn't have spent that sort of money on her. On the other hand, his concept of a lot of money would be quite different from hers.

Unconsciously touching a finger to the cross, she said, "I have no idea. The necklace was a gift."

Sage's brows shot up. "Your birthday won't be for several months. Who—?"

Thankfully, the bell sounded, giving Mariah the perfect excuse to leave Sage's question dangling. "Gotta run. See you later."

Back on Stallion Canyon, Finn was finishing the last of his lunch on the patio. Across from him, Harry's nanny had taken a seat in one of the wicker chairs and settled the baby comfortably in her lap.

This morning when he and Harry had returned from town, Finn had found Linda Baskin already here and waiting to take over her duties of caring for Harry. A tall, slender woman with a long blond ponytail threaded with streaks of gray, she appeared to be somewhere in her midfifties. Her complexion was ruddy and weather-beaten, her brown eyes crinkled at the corners. For the most part she was quiet and reserved, but friendly enough.

Last night, Finn had tried to convince Mariah that the nanny was no longer needed. He could certainly take care of Harry while she was at work. But Mariah wouldn't hear of it. She'd argued that he'd be wanting to spend time outdoors with the horses and he couldn't do that with a baby on his hip.

Yet now that Finn had met Linda, he realized that Mariah's reasoning to keep the nanny around was much more complex than giving him free time with the horses. The woman was totally enamored with Harry. Another fact that nagged at Finn. Linda would also be lost whenever he took his son home to the Horn.

Picking up a glass of iced tea, he leaned back in his chair and crossed his boots at the ankles. "Have you known the Montgomerys long?" Finn ventured to ask her.

"Twenty years or more," she said. "I met Ray and the girls when they first moved here. We all went to the same church, you see."

The baby was chewing his fist, while a stream of drool dripped from his chin. Last night Mariah had rubbed a soothing gel over his gums and predicted the tooth would be appearing soon. He wanted to be around to see Harry's first tooth appear and the many other firsts the child would have. But then, so did Mariah.

And this woman, too. Until this moment, Finn had never stopped to think about the connections a child created to all the people around him or her.

"That's a long time," Finn commented.

She handed Harry the green teething ring that Finn had purchased for him yesterday. The baby immediately jammed the piece of plastic in his mouth.

"I watched the girls grow up and Ray work to make this ranch into a fine home." She turned a wistful look toward the barns. "I never thought he'd die like he did. But then life is unpredictable, isn't it?"

Something in Linda's quiet voice told Finn that she was more than just a family acquaintance to the Montgomerys.

"That's why we should enjoy every day," he said, then asked, "Did you know Mariah is selling the ranch? She's already sold the horses to me."

With her gaze still on the barns, she said in a flat voice, "Yes, I know about the ranch. And the horses, too."

Finn had been wondering if Mariah had anyone close that she could talk to about private matters. Obviously Linda was that person.

"What do you think about her decision? About the ranch, that is."

"If it wasn't for her, this place would've already been sold through a sheriff's auction. She's gone as far as she can go. I don't like it. But that's the way it is. For now, at least."

Finn gazed thoughtfully toward the paddock where the mares were pastured. Beyond it, a ridge of forest-covered mountains curved toward the east. He figured with a bit of rain the foothills would hold some hearty grasses.

"Such a shame," he said thoughtfully. "I haven't seen much more than this area around the ranch yard, but what I see is beautiful."

Her features were stern as she looked at him. "Why don't you buy it?"

For a moment Finn was too stunned to know how to answer. "Me? I live on my family's ranch. I don't need this one."

She frowned. "Some men are independent and some aren't. I took you for the independent sort. But then, I'm not always right about people."

Finn had never expected to be having this sort of conversation with Harry's nanny, but now that she'd opened up, he couldn't resist the chance to find out more about Mariah's family.

"Now that we're on the subject, what sort of man was Ray Montgomery?" he asked.

A soft light entered the woman's brown eyes. It was the sort of look that was born from deep affection.

"A good, simple man. This ranch, the horses and his girls. That's all that mattered—all he wanted."

"Did you ever meet his ex-wife?"

Her brown eyes suddenly squinted. "That's a strange thing for you to be asking."

Finn shrugged. "I'm trying to get an idea of Harry's maternal family. Especially since they seem to be out of the picture. Mariah tells me her mother lives in Florida, but she never sees her."

She sighed. "Selma decided she didn't care for country life. She left the family long before Ray and the girls moved here. And that's the way it's stayed."

Finn tried to imagine his own mother leaving her

children behind, but it was impossible. Up until the day she'd died, Fiona had loved her five sons utterly.

"It takes a strong woman to be a rancher's wife," Finn mused aloud. "But why turn her back on her daughters?"

Harry began to fuss and squirm, prompting Linda to lift the baby to her shoulder and gently pat his back. "Because the girls wanted to live with their father and Selma never forgave her daughters for making that choice."

"Mariah hasn't mentioned ever having a stepmother around. Guess Ray never remarried."

The stark expression that spread over Linda's face spoke volumes to Finn.

"No," she said. "He remained single until he died."

Feeling as though he'd opened a diary that he had no right reading, Finn rose to his feet and gathered up the leftovers from his lunch. After putting the things away in the kitchen, he returned to the patio and picked up his hat.

"Going back to the barns?" Linda asked.

He tugged the brim of the felt low onto his forehead. "I have horses saddled and ready to be exercised."

"Be safe with those mustangs, Finn. I don't think Mariah could survive if you had an accident."

Finn stared at her. Was Linda trying to imply that Mariah cared for him? The idea was ridiculous. Sure, she'd kissed him as though she liked it. But that hardly meant she had feelings for him.

He chuckled sardonically. "Mariah isn't all that interested in my safety. In fact, she doesn't much care for men who wears spurs. And there's no chance of me ever taking mine off."

Before Linda could make any response, Finn left the patio and headed quickly toward the barns.

* * *

Later that evening when Mariah returned home from work, she dropped her tote and handbag on the coffee table, then walked straight to the middle of the living room where Linda had spread a blanket on the floor in front of the television. She was sitting cross-legged with Harry lying on his belly next to her. The baby was doing his best to get traction with his toes and push himself forward.

Bending down, she picked him up and cuddled him tightly against her shoulder. "How is my little man?" she crooned to the baby.

"Give him two or three more months and he'll probably be sitting on his own and crawling everywhere." She studied Mariah's drawn face. "You look drained. School must have been tough today."

"No more than usual." Closing her eyes, Mariah pressed her cheek against the top of Harry's head and tried to swallow away the tightness in her throat. The DNA test was off to the lab. Whether Finn was the father or not, once the results were determined, her life and Harry's would never be the same. The idea left a perpetual knot in the pit of her stomach.

Rising to her feet, Linda patted her shoulder. "It's Monday. Tomorrow will be better. Want a glass of tea or something?"

"Maybe later. I need to change clothes. Uh—how did you get on with Finn?"

"We understand each other, I think," Linda said, then gestured in the direction of the open doorway. "He's been down at the barns since lunch. I hope you're right about him being a horseman. That stallion isn't safe to be around and it's been four hours since I've seen him."

Concern fluttered in the pit of Mariah's stomach. Finn might be an expert horseman, but that didn't rule out accidents happening. "Finn should be able to handle himself around Rimrock. But I'd better go check on him just the same."

Mariah handed the baby over to Linda and quickly left the room. Once she reached the hallway, she didn't bother going to her bedroom to change out of her dress clothes. Instead, she exited the house through the kitchen and made a beeline to the main horse barn.

Along the way, her gaze desperately searched the ranch yard for a sign of Finn. As crazy as it seemed, he'd already become a part of her life. The image of him lying in the dirt, hurt or worse, sent a rush of icy fear through her. If something had happened to him, she'd be devastated.

Quickening her steps, Mariah reached the shed row where the stallion, Rimrock, was stalled along with four geldings. The gates to all five stalls were swung wide with no horses to be seen. A hurried glance told her the stalls had been shoveled all the way to the dirt floor, but no clean shavings had yet been added. At the far end of the shed row, near the tack room, a shoeing stand, a rasp and hoof nippers were lying on the ground.

Finn had certainly been busy. That much was clear. But where was he now? A glance at the paddock to her right told her the mares were all there, munching contentedly at a manger full of alfalfa.

Suddenly the wind swirled from the north and with it came a cloud of dust from the other side of the barn. Mariah hurried around the huge building, then stopped in her tracks and stared in amazement at the training arena some fifty yards away.

Finn was riding Rimrock in a slow lope, directing the horse in large looping figure eights. Dust boiled from the stallion's hoofs, sending brown clouds swirling around animal and rider.

Slower now, she walked over to the arena and stood just outside the wire mesh fence to watch. Finn was handling Rimrock as though he was a docile kid pony, instead of a high-strung stallion that hadn't had a person on his back since her father had passed away.

Only a few moments clicked by before Finn spotted her. With a short wave, he drew Rimrock to a walk and directed the horse in her direction. As horse and rider grew closer, she noticed Finn was wearing a pair of hard-worn chinks with hand-sewn buck stitching. The butterscotch-colored leather was scratched and scarred from the top of his thighs all the way down to his knees, while in some spots the fringe edging the legs was either missing or broken off to a shorter length. A pair of long shanked spurs with clover rowels worn smooth on the edges were strapped to his boots. Apparently he carried the tools of his trade with him at all times, she decided.

One thing for certain, no matter what angle Mariah looked at him from, he was all cowboy. And the sight of him sitting astride Rimrock was more than enough to set her heart to pounding.

"Hey, Mariah," he greeted her with a grin. "How was school today?"

Beneath the shade of his broad-brimmed hat, she could see his gaze traveling up and down the length of her. No doubt he was wondering why she was out here in the dusty ranch yard in a skirt and high heels. But she wasn't about to confess she was so worried about him she'd hurried straight out here instead of changing clothes.

Her heart suddenly hammering, she struggled to tuck strands of loosened hair back into the twist at the back of her head. "School was fine. From the looks of the stalls you've been busy today."

The saddle leather creaked as Rimrock took a restless side step. Finn gently touched his spur into the horse's side to make him return to the spot where he'd initially reined him to a stop.

"I've been occupied."

He rested a forearm across the horn of the saddle and Mariah could see he was as much at home on a horse as he was in a chair at the breakfast table.

She said, "In case you hadn't found them, the clean shavings are in the tractor shed."

"I found the shavings. But I'm in no hurry to spread them. I'm going to turn the horses out for a while. They need to graze and run. And they especially need to socialize with one another."

Mariah spluttered. "You're letting them loose? I hope you're not planning to put the geldings in with Rimrock. He's wild. He might kill them!"

Finn chuckled and Mariah's backbone immediately stiffened. Aimee had often laughed at her, too. Her sister had considered Mariah's knowledge concerning horses, and men, and fashion, amusing and even more lacking. It hurt to think that Finn considered her naive, too.

"He doesn't appear wild to me." He patted the stallion's neck. "Besides, the geldings have legs. If need be, they'll scoot out of his way. But Rimrock understands the geldings are not—uh, let's just say, all men. So he hardly feels threatened by their presence."

Shading her eyes with her hand, she continued to gaze up at him. "Dad was the last person to ride Rimrock four years ago. He was very unruly then. How did you get him to behave like this?"

A slow grin exposed his teeth and it struck Mariah that she'd spent half the day dreaming about those lips, while the other half had been on Harry. She could only hope she'd made sense while she'd been lecturing her students on California history.

"I just told him we were going to be buddies. That's all."

He climbed down from the horse and came to stand directly in front of Mariah. The fence between them did nothing to protect her senses from his overwhelming presence, and with each passing moment she felt her breaths grow slower and her heart beat faster.

"That simple, huh?"

He grinned and the warm light in his eyes sent pleasure spreading through her like a ray of sun after a long, cold rain. Being away from him only for a few hours had seemed like an eternity, and now that he was standing so near, it was all she could do to keep from reaching through the fence and latching onto his shirt. Just to touch him in any small way gave her pleasure. The kind of pleasure that was hard to resist.

"I've been riding since I was just a wee tot. And everyone tells me that I have a kinship with horses. I'm sure your dad had it, too."

Ray Montgomery had been a good horseman, but he'd had to work hard to learn the trade. Mariah figured it all came natural to Finn. As natural as the dimples in his cheeks and the easy way his lips had moved over hers.

In an effort to clear her straying thoughts, she drew

in a deep breath and blew it out. "A tot? Exactly how old were you when you took your first ride?"

"I'm told my grandfather carried me in the saddle when I was only a few weeks old."

"A few weeks! Your mother must've been going out of her mind with fear!"

Chuckling, he said, "Not really. She'd already seen my three older brothers on a horse when they were only babies. By the time I came along, she was used to it."

"So this means if Harry turns out to be your son, you'll be putting him on the back of a horse in the near future?"

His grin deepened. "No 'ifs,' Mariah. Only when. And once the test reveals I'm the father, then I plan on doing lots of things with Harry. And that includes riding him on a gentle horse."

Even though the idea of Harry being on the back of a thousand-pound animal was terrifying, she didn't say anything. Because in the end, if it turned out that Harry was his son, she'd have no rights to the child's upbringing.

After a stretch of silence, he asked, "What? No loud protest?"

"No." She smoothed a hand down the front of her skirt, then turned away from him. "And now that I see you haven't been kicked in the head or bucked off with a broken leg, I'd better be getting back to the house. I'm keeping Linda from going home."

He arched a brow at her. "Oh. So you were worried about me?"

Heat flared in her cheeks. "Linda said she hadn't seen you since lunch. We were both concerned."

A sly glint appeared in his blue eyes. "It's nice to have a woman worrying over me."

"I'm not worried now." She turned to go only to have him reach through the fence and snag a hold of her shoulder.

"Wait, Mariah. Before you leave, I want to talk to you. Let me tie Rimrock and I'll come around there," he told her.

Finn tethered Rimrock to a post, then exited the arena through a nearby gate. As he walked down the fence to where Mariah stood, he was struck by how different she looked. Compared to the blue jeans and work shirts he'd seen her in the past two days, she looked far different in a slim gray skirt and thin white blouse. Although the feminine clothes were cut modestly, her curves filled them out in all the right ways. And the black high heels covering her pretty little feet were as sexy as all get-out.

Halting a short space away from her, he tried not to gawk, but ever since they'd parted ways at the health department this morning, he hadn't been able to get her image out of his mind. Now his eyes seemed to have a mind of their own. Instead of looking out at the mountains or the mares behind her shoulder, they continued to travel over her mussed black hair, the thrust of her breasts and the enticing way her hips curved out from her tiny waist.

"You have something you want to say?" she asked.

Clearing his throat, he said, "Uh—yes, the fences— I wanted to ask you about them."

"What about the fences?"

The fabric of her blouse was just sheer enough to

show a hint of lacy undergarment, and the sight stirred up thoughts that he'd been trying all day to forget.

With a mental shake of his head, he gestured toward the open land to the west. "Do you know if the fences are upright? And is the land sectioned off with cross fences? I'll need to know before I let the horses out to pasture. I don't want them wandering too far away from the ranch yard or getting on your neighbor's land."

A thoughtful frown furrowed her brow. "Sorry. I don't know how long it's been since the fences have been inspected. Dad used to make routine checks to ensure they were all intact. But after he died Aimee wasn't too concerned about fences. All she ever worried about was the arena and the stalls."

"That's a hell of a way to run a ranch," he said frankly.

One of her slender shoulders made a negligible shrug and the movement drew Finn's gaze to the white fabric opened at her throat. The silver cross he'd given her was lying against her creamy skin and he found himself wondering if she was wearing the piece of jewelry because she liked it, or the man who'd given it to her?

She said, "Looking back on it now, after Dad died we should have hired a man to manage the ranch. He might've done a better job than me of dealing with Aimee's neglectful ways."

"No use fretting about the past now. I'll check the fences myself. I'm sure there are a few old roads traveling over parts of the ranch. I'll drive out this evening and inspect what I can before dark. Would you like to go with me?"

Her lips parted and Finn's gaze homed in on the moist curve of her lower lip. He'd kissed plenty of girls over the years, but none of them had tasted quite as sweet or seductive as Mariah. And that was worrisome. How did a man forget something that good?

"I suppose I could join you," she said guardedly. "But what about Harry? I'd have to ask Linda to stay and watch him."

She was being agreeable and that was enough to put a grin on his face. "No need for that. The weather is nice. We'll take him with us. Isn't that what parents do when they go on a family outing—take their baby with them?"

Confusion flickered in her eyes. "But we're not parents."

Unable to stop himself, Finn moved closer and gently cupped his hand along the side of her face. "For now we're Harry's parents," he said softly.

"Yes. I suppose. For now."

Her eyes suddenly misted over and before he could say anything else, she pulled away from him.

As Finn watched her walk away, he realized the taste of Mariah's lips wasn't only one thing he'd eventually have to forget about the woman. The depth of emotion in her gray eyes, the touch of her hand, the heady scent of her skin and the sweet husky lilt in her voice. Those things would haunt Finn long after he was back on the Horn and Mariah had moved on with her life.

Did that mean he was falling in love with her?

Hell, Finn, that's a stupid question. You've only known Mariah for three days. A man can't lose his heart to a woman that quickly.

Maybe not, Finn thought uneasily. But a moment ago when she'd walked away with tears in her eyes, he'd felt like a part of him had gone with her.

Chapter Eight

For now we're Harry's parents.

Later that evening as Finn drove the three of them over the western section of the ranch, his words continued to roll through Mariah's thoughts. To imagine the two of them as Harry's parents, even temporary ones, was bittersweet.

As a young girl growing up without a mother, and with a father who'd been absorbed in his work, Mariah had dreamed of having a real family of her own. One that was loving and whole and could never be torn apart. When she'd met Kris during her college studies, she'd thought all those dreams were going to come true. Dark-haired and conservative in nature, he'd been the first guy who'd given her a serious glance and she'd naively fallen for his attention. Now she realized what a Pollyanna she'd been to trust him. Even more to believe in her dreams. Real families were fairy tales. At least, in her world they were.

But with Finn sitting only inches away and Harry safely ensconced in his car carrier in the backseat, she couldn't stop herself from dreaming, or smiling.

For nearly an hour Finn drove the truck alongside a network of boundary and cross fences that were located closest to the ranch yard. Once he'd determined the repairs needed, he decided to follow a dim, overgrown road that would lead them to a portion of the ranch that ran alongside a river.

Eventually, the truck crested a small rise and a stretch of open land lay before them. In spite of the dry spring, the ground was covered with clumps of grass and long-stemmed yellow flowers that bowed with the evening breeze.

Finn braked the truck to a stop to take in the sight. "Oh, Mariah, this is awesome," Finn declared. "I'm going to guess this is the area where your father grew alfalfa."

She nodded. "That's right. And about a mile on west from here is a second meadow that was used for grass hay. There's some of the irrigation system over there." She pointed to their left, where long pipes connected to large spoke wheels sat at the edge of the tree line. The weeds growing around the equipment revealed how long it had been sitting idle.

"Did your dad pump water from the river or is there a well around here somewhere?"

"Both. Depending on how much irrigating he wanted to do. The well is somewhere over there by the wheel line."

"Let's get out of the truck for a better look," he suggested. "We'll leave the doors open and stay right by the truck so we can keep an eye on Harry."

"All right."

The jostling of the truck had lulled Harry into a deep sleep. Mariah covered him with a light blanket to protect him from the cool evening air before Finn helped her to the ground.

Once they were standing together at the side of the truck, Mariah gazed around her and drank in the beauty of the nearby mountains juxtaposed with flat river land. Other than the faint sounds of insects and the rustle of leaves, a peaceful silence encompassed them.

"I'd almost forgotten how beautiful it is here," she murmured. "When Aimee and I were small we used to ride horses to this meadow. In the summer we'd take off our boots and wade in the river. 'Course, we never told Dad about the wading," she added with a wistful smile.

Finn moved close enough to slip an arm around the back of her waist. The warm weight of it filled her with an odd mixture of contentment and excitement.

"So you did have some good times here on the ranch."

Pleasant memories suddenly flooded through her, causing her heart to wince. "Lots of them," she said lowly. "But that was before Aimee and I grew apart. And before Dad left us."

He looked down at her, his eyes full of misgivings. "I wish you'd change your mind about selling the ranch, Mariah."

"Why?"

His hand tightened on the side of her waist. "Because I have a feeling and it's telling me you belong here."

Her rueful laugh came out sounding more like a

choked sob. "You don't know me well enough to make that call."

With hands on both sides of her waist, he turned her toward him. Mariah's heart thumped with anticipation.

"I've already learned a lot about you, Mariah. There are so many things I can see in your eyes that tell me what you're thinking and the kind of woman you are."

Unable to stop herself, she rested her palms against his chest. "And what sort of woman am I?" she asked huskily.

His head bent toward hers until a scant space was the only thing separating their lips.

"A woman I want to see smile. A woman I want to make love to."

By the time his voice died away, his lips were hovering over hers, robbing her breath and her senses.

"Finn," she whispered.

His arms tightened around her. "Tell me you want me, Mariah. As much as I want you."

His words were enough to make her tremble. "I do want you, Finn. Very much."

She heard him groan and then everything else faded away as he began to kiss her. Not in a gentle way. But in a hungry, all-consuming way that weakened her knees and forced her fists to snatch hold of the front of his shirt.

Just when she was certain she was going to faint from lack of oxygen, Finn lifted his head. But the reprieve only lasted long enough for her to haul in one deep breath before his mouth attacked hers once again from a different angle.

A tiny particle of Mariah's brain recognized that something was happening between her and Finn. Something that went far beyond the heat fusing their mouths together. She wanted to tear his clothes away, to beg him to make love to her right here on the ground.

The reckless abandon racing through her was like lightning racing across a summer sky. And when his hand cupped her breasts and his mouth made a downward descent along her neck, she groaned with raw, unleashed desire.

It wasn't until he'd unbuttoned the top of her blouse and pressed his lips against the valley between her breasts that a brief flash of sanity warned her to end the embrace. But the pleasure of Finn touching her, wanting her, was something she'd never had before. She couldn't give it up.

Nearby, a night bird suddenly called. Then called again. The sound must have shaken Finn out of the erotic fog that had wrapped around them. He lifted his head, then eased back far enough to allow the cool night air to drift between them.

Totally shaken, Mariah turned and attempted to catch her breath and wrangle her scattered senses back together.

Behind her, she could hear the ragged intake of Finn's breath and she wondered if his world was tilting as much as hers. Or was making love to a woman second nature to him? It had certainly felt like it, she thought.

"Dusk is falling," Finn said after a moment. "Are you ready to head back to the ranch?"

The fact that he was giving her a choice to leave this magical place made her feel somewhat more in control of herself, but only a little.

She cleared her throat. "Yes. I—think we'd better."

He moved up behind her and closed a hand over her

shoulder. "I can't apologize for any of that, Mariah," he said gently. "When I touch you it feels very special. Not like something I should be ashamed of."

Her eyes squeezed tight, she fought against the urge to turn and fling herself back into his arms. Oh, how good it would feel to let herself go, to simply enjoy this man's touch without worrying about tomorrow. She deserved that, didn't she? To simply allow herself to be a woman?

Trembling through and through, she turned and gave him a wobbly smile. "It feels very special to me, too, Finn. But I'm not sure if it's the right thing for me. I don't do this sort of thing for fun and games."

"That didn't feel like a game to me."

She could find no appropriate reply to that, and with a hand at her back, he urged her around to the truck.

On the way back to the ranch, Mariah remained quiet and so did Finn. The episode at the meadow had swiftly altered everything between them. Now as she gazed out at the darkening landscape it was as though she were seeing it for the first time. The same way her father must have seen it twenty years ago. And the images put a very real pang of loss in her heart.

Much later that night Mariah woke up without reason and glanced at the digital clock on the nightstand: 1:20 a.m. She groaned. For hours she'd lain awake, reliving Finn's every touch, every word, until finally sleep had overtaken her mind. Why had she suddenly woken? Had she been dreaming?

The quietness of the house settled around her at the same time an uneasy sensation pricked her senses. Something was wrong.

Tossing back the covers, she rapidly tied a light robe

over her gown and hurried across the hallway to Harry's nursery. Beneath the dim glow of the night-light, she could see the baby was sleeping soundly and she sent up a prayer of relief.

Still, something didn't feel right, and that perception deepened when she walked down the hall and saw the door to Finn's room standing wide open. As a respect to her privacy and his, he always kept the door shut whenever he was in his bedroom. Seeing it open and the room dark meant one thing. He wasn't there.

Panic suddenly struck her and she raced on bare feet out to the kitchen. A night-light next to the sink illuminated the room enough for her to see that Finn wasn't there. And with the rest of the house in darkness that could only mean he was outside.

Grabbing up her cowboy boots from the mudroom, she jerked them on and dashed out the back door. The temperature had fallen drastically since she'd gone to bed, but she hardly noticed the chill as she instinctively ran toward the barns.

Lights were burning beneath the shed row, but Finn wasn't anywhere in sight.

Slowing to a trot, she glanced into each stall. By the time she reached the end, Finn was still nowhere in sight.

Pausing to give the frantic beating of her heart a chance to catch up, she called loudly, "Finn? Where are you?"

"Over here, Mariah."

Relieved, she followed the sound of his voice to the back of the barn where a small pen was equipped with a lean-to shelter. Beneath the overhang of the tin roof, she could see the shadowy image of Finn kneeling over a downed horse. Her short-lived relief was suddenly pierced with alarm and she quickly let herself into the enclosure.

"Finn, what's wrong?"

"I came out here to check on the mares before I went to bed. Thank God I did. This one is trying to foal. But both of the baby's front feet are together. The head won't follow that way. One foot needs to be forward more."

"Oh, no! This is her first foal, Finn. Should I call the vet?"

"I've already called one. But it'll probably be another hour before he can get here." Finn gently rubbed the mare's sweaty flank. "I've got to do something before then or it will be too late for both of them."

Mariah could hardly bear to hear the animal's groans as she strained to expel the baby from her. She'd never helped with any of the foaling before. Her father had taken care of those things. Along with Aimee's help. Mariah had always been told her help wasn't needed. "Is there anything I can do?"

He glanced up, his gaze making a rapid sweep over her. "You're going to freeze in those nightclothes. And what about Harry?"

"Harry is sound asleep in his crib."

His expression stern, he said, "I don't want him left in the house alone. You'd better get back."

"I'm not leaving you out here unaided," she practically shouted. "You might need help before the vet arrives."

Rising to his full height to emphasize his point, he repeated, "I said I don't want Harry in the house alone!"

Seeing that there was no point in arguing the matter, she started out of the pen. "Fine," she muttered. "We'll do this your way."

Not waiting to hear his response, she left the barn area and hurried to the house. Inside, she pulled a jean jacket over her robe, then went straight to the nursery and gently swaddled Harry in a heavy quilt. The child never stirred. Even when she made a beeline back to the barns.

After she'd settled the sleeping baby in his wagon, she positioned it in a safe position outside the mare's pen.

By now, Finn was too involved with the troubled delivery to notice her whereabouts, until she reentered the pen and joined him beneath the overhang.

"I brought Harry back with me. He's sound asleep and warmly bundled," she told him, then gestured toward the straining mare. "Is she any better?"

Finn dismally shook his head. "No. And too much time has already passed. I'm going to try one more thing to see if the baby will turn itself. If it doesn't, then I'll have to try to do it myself."

She drew in a sharp breath. "Have you done that sort of thing before?"

"Only a handful of times. Mostly, there's no need. The Horn has a resident vet that handles the ranch's emergencies."

The evident worry on his face urged Mariah to lay a reassuring hand on his shoulder. "If you've done it before you can do it again. I have every faith in you. But let's pray you won't have to."

He shot her a grateful look. "I don't want to lose this mare and baby. Right now I've got to get her up and walking. Hopefully that might relieve enough pressure of the uterine walls to give the foal enough room to turn itself."

Mariah moved out of the way and Finn wasted no

time in getting the suffering mare to her feet and walking her around and around the small pen. Five minutes passed, then ten. All the while Mariah continued to pray for the mare's and baby's safety.

Eventually the mare balked and started lowering herself back to the ground. Finn dropped his hold on the lead rope and allowed her to stretch out.

"Finn! What's happening? Is she dying?" Mariah asked frantically.

Finn knelt closer to the mare and began to examine her. "No. I think she's telling us the baby will come out now. Yes! Here it comes! Just the way it should."

Mariah watched in wonder as first one little hoof emerged. A few inches behind, the second hoof appeared, and then the head. After that, the mare had no trouble delivering the rest of the foal.

For the next half hour, Mariah watched Finn deftly deal with the pair, who appeared to be in good condition, especially considering the prolonged birth. When the lights of a vehicle announced the arrival of the vet, she scooped up Harry.

"The vet's here," she told Finn. "I don't want him to see me in my nightclothes. I'm going back to the house."

As she started off, he called to her. She paused long enough for him to walk over to her.

"Yes?"

A crooked grin twisted his weary features. "Thank you."

His tender words of appreciation added to the incredibly tense moments they'd shared over the mare all came together at once to cause Mariah's eyes to mist over. "I didn't do anything," she said.

"Just being here was exactly what I needed."

Her heart melting, she touched his hand and then scurried back to the house.

* * *

Another hour and a half passed before the vet finished administering care to the new mother and baby. Once the doctor packed up and drove away, Finn walked slowly back to the house.

He should've been dog tired. He'd been at the barn for hours and the fear of losing the mare and baby had been worse than stressful. But the joyous outcome had wiped all his weariness away. Now, in spite of his watch reading close to three in the morning, he was wide-awake.

When he reached the back door, a light was on in the kitchen. But when he stepped inside and spotted Mariah sitting at the breakfast bar, he was more than surprised.

"It's late," he said. "You should be in bed."

He hung his hat and jacket on a hall tree located a few steps away from the door. When he turned back around, Mariah was standing in front of him, her pale face strained, yet hopeful.

"The mare and baby?" she asked anxiously.

She honestly and truly cared. The realization filled him with incredible joy. "Both fine. The filly is already on her feet and nursing."

She let out a tiny groan of relief and then suddenly she was wrapping her arms around his neck and burying her face in his chest.

"Oh, Finn. I was so worried about you—and them."

Finn didn't bother to wait or wonder what had brought on this show of affection. She was holding him, touching him as though she never wanted to let him go. And that was all that mattered. With a hand beneath her chin, he tilted her mouth up to his and kissed her hard and quick. "Mariah, my sweet. Before I went out to check on the mares, I was fighting myself to keep from going to your bedroom."

Pink color stained her cheeks and he kissed the soft, heated skin while his nostrils pulled in the sweet, musky scent of her hair. Having her in his arms was like an incredible dream, one that he wanted to remember long after it ended.

"And I was lying awake," she whispered. "Hoping you would."

"And now?" he asked.

"Now all I can think about is being next to you. Like this."

Groaning deep in his throat, he lifted her into his arms and carried her straight to her bedroom.

The room was dark, but a yard lamp outside the window slanted strips of faint light across the bed and floor. The rumpled bedcovers exposed a wide expanse of white sheet.

Finn placed her in the middle of the bed, then stood staring down at her, allowing himself a moment to let his mind catch up with desire that was already gripping his body.

"I washed my hands at the barn," was all he could manage to utter. "But my clothes are dirty."

She pushed herself to a sitting position and reached for him. "I don't care about that," she whispered. "I'm going to take them off you anyway."

Her boldness sent a thrill of anticipation through him, and when her hands grabbed his belt and tugged him forward, he went willingly down beside her.

Wrapping his arms around her, he pulled her tight against him and pressed his lips to the middle of her forehead. "I can't believe this is happening," he mouthed against her. "After we came home from the meadow you were—so withdrawn. I was sure you were wishing you could wipe out everything that had happened with us."

Her hands came up to cradle his face. "I wasn't re-gretting, Finn. I was thinking. About myself. And you. I don't want to be afraid anymore. Afraid to let myself make love to you—to let myself be a woman."

Emotions he didn't quite understand poured into him and suddenly he felt as though he was ten feet tall and walking on air.

"Mariah, my sweet."

Finding her lips, he began to kiss her deeply, his mouth searching for the same wild excitement he'd felt when they'd kissed in the meadow. And he wasn't dis-appointed as it crashed into his head as quick as thunder after a violent flash of lightning.

Desire hummed along his veins as she opened the front of his shirt, then flattened her palms against his heated skin. While his lips continued to devour hers, he felt her fingers begin a search of their own. They lingered at his flat nipples, then slid to the small of his back before coming to rest on the waistband of his jeans.

Tearing his mouth away from hers, he climbed off the bed and started stripping away his clothing.

Mariah levered herself up on one elbow and watched him peel off a pair of navy blue boxer shorts. "I was going to do that," she complained.

"Next time, baby. We'll go slower. Right now I can't wait to touch you—get inside you."

With his clothing lying in a heap on the floor, he leaned over her to remove her gown and robe. Once they were tossed over his shoulder, he rejoined her on the bed, where she immediately rolled into him and swung her leg over his hips.

The sensation of her warm flesh touching his robbed his breath, and suddenly the pleasures attacking his senses were almost overwhelming. He wanted to taste her lips, her breasts, every curve and nuance of her body. He wanted to touch and hold and feel her soft skin sliding against his.

He'd torn his mouth from hers and was circling his mouth around one pert nipple when her fingers slid into his hair and gently tugged to garner his attention.

Tilting his head back, he saw that her gray eyes were half closed, her long black hair fanned against the white sheet. The swollen curves of her lips beckoned him. But then, so did the rest of her body, and he wanted to explore every inch of it. But if she was having reservations, he'd have to find the strength to get up and walk out of the room.

His throat thick, he shoved out the question. "Is something wrong?"

"No. But I think I should tell you that I haven't done this—well, in a long, long time."

Shifting slightly away from her, he propped his head on one hand and used the other to gently push a curtain of tangled waves from the side of her face. Uncertainty darkened her eyes, and the corner of her lips trembled.

Her vulnerability pierced him and all he wanted at that moment was to protect and reassure her. "Sweetheart, don't be scared. I'll be as gentle as you want me to be."

Her head moved back and forth against the mattress. "That's not worrying me," she mumbled. "I'm inexperienced. And I...just don't want to disappoint you."

Groaning with disbelief, Finn cradled her head against the curve of his neck. "Oh, darling, you couldn't do that. Having you in my arms—loving me. That's all I need from you." Tilting her head back, he traced a fingertip across her cheekbone. "Do I need to wear protection?"

Relief eased the tension on her face. "I'm on oral birth control. But maybe you'd feel safer with more protection—I won't mind."

Oddly enough, the idea of creating a baby with Mariah felt natural and right to him. What did that mean? That he was too full of lust to care? Or that Mariah had already become very, very special to him?

Squeezing those questions to the far fringes of his mind, Finn kissed her softly. "I don't need to feel safe. Not with you."

He heard the soft intake of her breath and then everything faded away as he brought his lips down on hers and her arms wrapped tightly around him.

He kissed her until his breath was gone and he was forced to tear his mouth away. While his lungs gorged themselves on oxygen, his hands made a sweeping exploration of her curves. Over her breasts, down her rib cage and across her flat belly. And then finally, the heated juncture between her thighs.

When he touched her there, she moaned and arched against him, inviting his fingers to slip inside. The slick warmth made his loins ache with need, and though he wanted to linger and enjoy each sensation to the fullest, his body refused to wait.

Rolling her onto her back, he poised himself over her and in the semidarkness of the room, her gaze locked with his. The connection sent a shock of awareness through him and suddenly he was almost afraid to make the final, ultimate link with her. Because he understood it would be irrevocable and life changing.

"Finn." As she breathed his name, the upper part of her body lifted from the mattress and molded itself against his. "Don't think. Or worry. Or make me wait another second," she pleaded.

Even if he'd wanted to, he couldn't turn back now. His heart, mind and soul were screaming for the chance to absorb her sweetness, to draw in the very essence of her being and hold it fast inside him.

"Mariah."

Her name was but a whisper as he blindly thrust himself into her welcoming body. Delicious heat instantly wrapped around him, rocking him with vibrations of pleasure so intense that his teeth snapped together.

Beneath him, Mariah's hips shifted upward, drawing him deeper within her. The movement was very nearly his undoing, but after a steadying breath, he regained enough control to begin a steady thrust.

Hot. Sweet. Perfect. On and on it went until his mind no longer belonged to him. At some point Mariah had taken control of his every movement, every thought that entered his brain. He'd become a willing prisoner and he never wanted her lips to release his, her arms to let go. If there was such a place as paradise, she was quickly leading him straight to it.

Somewhere in the back of his mind, he registered her soft moans and the frantic foray her hands were making upon his chest, across his belly and buttocks. Each touch of her fingers, each kiss of her lips upon his skin, scorched him, tightened every cell in his body until blood was roaring in his ears and his gasps for air were harsh and rapid.

"Finn. Oh, Finn."

The sound of his name coming from her lips was all it took to break the last fragile thread of his control. With his hands clenching her buttocks, he held her hips tight against his until a burst of light exploded behind his eyes and suddenly he was breaking into tiny pieces. The ragged bits flew to the ceiling, then floated aimlessly around the dark room before they finally settled slowly back to his sated, sweaty body.

Yet even after the axis of his world righted itself, Finn recognized that a part of him was now missing. And he had the very real and scary feeling that the lost piece of him was his heart.

Chapter Nine

Three days later, Mariah was in her classroom, gathering the books and papers scattered across the desk top. Less than five minutes ago, the final bell for the day had sounded and the students had scattered out the door. Except for tall, brown-haired Lucia. With a heavy backpack fastened to her shoulders and a sweater tied around her waist, the teenager paused at the corner of Mariah's desk.

"Did you need to talk to me about something, Lucia?"

Winding a finger through the end of her ponytail, the girl nervously chewed on her bottom lip. Mariah wished she had the right to give her a reassuring hug. Although Lucia made excellent grades, Mariah understood the girl's home life was not the best in the world.

"It's not about our assignment for tomorrow, Ms. Montgomery. I've just been wondering. Since school is almost out for summer...I mean...will you be coming back next fall?"

Next fall? For the past few days Mariah hadn't allowed herself to think too much about the future, even the near future. Enjoying the fleeting time she had with Finn was all that mattered. But Lucia's question was forcing her to picture the future and at this moment, it looked very uncertain.

Frowning thoughtfully, she asked, "What makes you ask that?"

The teenager blushed. "Well, uh, some of the kids have been saying that you're going to Nevada. I sure hope that isn't true, Ms. Montgomery. I'd really miss you."

Mariah had no idea how the rumor had gotten started about her going to Nevada. She didn't think Sage had spoken to anyone about it, but that day in the lounge when they'd been discussing the subject, someone could have overheard their conversation. Now apparently the rumor was all over the school.

Smiling at the girl, she reached for a tote bag. "Don't worry, Lucia. If I go to Nevada it will only be for a short visit. I'll be back for the next school year."

Grinning with relief, Lucia bounced on her toes. "That's great, Ms. Montgomery! Really great!"

Mariah smiled, then glanced pointedly at her wristwatch. "The bus will be leaving in a few minutes. You don't want to miss it."

"Oh! I gotta run!"

The teenager raced out of the room and Mariah thoughtfully began to load the tote bag with the things she needed to carry home.

Home to Stallion Canyon. Strange, how much that

image had changed in her mind. For the past few months, she'd thought of little else but selling the place and moving to a new home and a new life. She'd wholeheartedly believed everything would be better for her and Harry if the ranch was out of their lives once and for all.

But now that Finn was here, everything had changed. She was seeing the ranch as it had been years ago, a beautiful home where she'd lived and loved and laughed with her father and sister. And hope had begun to stir within her. Hope that the impossible might happen and she could somehow manage to keep Stallion Canyon.

Face it, Mariah. You've fallen in love with Finn. He's the reason Stallion Canyon looks so good to you now. With him living in your house and sleeping in your bed, the place feels perfect to you. But sooner or later, with or without Harry, he'll be leaving. And then what will you have? Besides a broken heart?

Mariah shoved a stack of tests papers into the tote and refused to let the mocking voice prick the happy thought of going home to Finn. The time would come soon enough to face the sad fact of losing her home, her baby and her man.

Back on Stallion Canyon, Finn sat in the kitchen, gently nudging the toe of his boot against the floor to keep the old rocking chair in motion. Harry had already finished a bottle and now his blue eyes were closed in sleep. Finn needed to rise and carry the boy to his crib, but each time he held Harry in his arms he was fascinated with his tiny features and the little hands that were already learning to grip. He loved feeling the baby's warm weight resting against his chest, while he dreamed of the day his son would become a man.

"Harry is going to be as tall as me, don't you think?"

Across the room, Linda continued to fold laundry atop the breakfast bar. "Probably. But do you ever wonder if you might be setting yourself up for a disappointment? It's not right to talk about the dead, but I have to say that Aimee was no angel."

Maybe she hadn't been perfect, Finn thought. But that hardly mattered anymore. Mariah was the only woman he could think about. Making love to her these past few nights had changed him. Now as he looked toward the future, he could see only her and Harry in his life. If that meant he'd fallen in love with her, he didn't know. He only knew that she'd become just as important to him as little Harry.

"The DNA isn't back yet. But Harry is mine," Finn said with confidence.

"Hmm, and then what? You'll be taking him home to Nevada?" she asked.

He hadn't expected Linda to prod him about his personal plans. At least not until they had complete confirmation of the baby's DNA. But considering the time and emotions the woman had invested in Harry, she had a right to ask.

"That's right. That's where my home is." He looked at her. "Why? You didn't think I'd be leaving him here, did you?"

She cast him a sly look. "Actually, I was thinking you might be considering making your home here. What with all the fencing and other work you've been doing around here, you'd think this was your ranch."

For the past four days, Finn had been working diligently to patch sagging wire and leaning fence posts so he'd have a secure pasture to turn out the geldings.

Or he'd told himself that was the reason. In truth, he should be making arrangements to get the horses and mares shipped back to Nevada. Instead, he wanted to find every excuse he could to keep them here, and more important, to keep himself here.

"I like keeping busy. And this place needs lots of work to get it back into shape."

Frowning, she picked up a towel and shook out the wrinkles. "So someone else can buy it?"

Finn looked down at the sleeping baby. In years to come, Stallion Canyon should be handed over to Harry, or at the very least shared with any children that Mariah might have in the future.

Mariah having children with some other man. The ranch being sold to a stranger. The thoughts were agonizing to Finn, and yet sooner rather than later, they were realities he would have to face.

He looked over to Linda. "The real estate agent called Mariah last night to let her know that two different men are interested in the property. One wants to harvest the timber on it. The other one wants to plow the meadows and grow potatoes."

Both ideas sickened Finn. Stallion Canyon was a wild, beautiful mixture of mountain ridges and valley floors that stretched along a narrow, winding river. It wasn't meant to be stripped of timber or plowed into fields. It was a land to raise horses, not lumber or vegetables.

Linda scowled. "I suppose they'll be coming out to look the place over. I hope I'm not here when either of them come. I—well, Ray is surely turning over in his grave. That's all I can say."

She picked up the basket and left the room. Finn rose to his feet and carried Harry to the nursery. As he carefully put the baby to bed, the whole situation gnawed at him like an empty stomach begging for a bite of food. Mariah, Harry and Stallion Canyon. This past week all three had begun to feel as though they belonged to him. Was he thinking liked a damned fool? Or was he thinking like a man who'd finally figured out what he wanted in life?

Back in Alturas, Mariah was about to leave the school parking lot when she spotted Sage hurrying toward the driver's side of her car.

Mariah pressed the button to lower the window. "What's wrong? Car won't start?"

Sage smiled. "No problems. I wanted to catch you—I thought we might stop by the Silver Slipper and have an ice cream together before you go home."

"You're a sweetheart to ask, but I really don't have the time. Linda will be expecting me."

Sage frowned. "All you have to do is pick up your cell and call her. I'm sure she wouldn't mind staying with Harry another thirty minutes. Besides, Harry's father is there. He can look after his son."

Yes, Finn was there. The fact made her heart smile. It made her want to rush home and spend every precious minute she could with him. "He's been staying pretty busy around the ranch. Besides working with the horses, he's been repairing fences and working on the irrigation pump."

Sage's expression turned to sly speculation. "Hmm. Why would Finn be doing all that? He'll be leaving soon and you're selling the ranch."

Actually, Mariah had been asking herself the very same things. She could understand the time and work he put in on the horses. They belonged to him. But the ranch was a different matter. Was he doing it for her? Because he knew she had no money or means to make upgrades to the property?

"Finn isn't the sort of man who can just sit around. He wants to keep busy."

Sage didn't look at all convinced, but mercifully dropped the subject.

"Well, call Linda," she said. "I'll meet you at the Slipper."

Assuming that Mariah would agree to follow, Sage turned away from the window to leave.

Mariah called out to her. "Sage, I don't have time. It's not just keeping Linda overtime. I have—things to do. Supper to cook for Finn."

Sage's brows shot up. "Oh? Sounds like this whole thing has turned into a family situation to me."

Mariah sheepishly glanced away from Sage's inquisitive face. If her friend only knew how she'd been making love to Finn these past few nights, she'd be properly shocked. But nothing about sharing her bed with Finn felt shocking. It felt right and special. And though she was probably crazy for thinking of her and Finn and Harry as a family, she couldn't help it.

"So what if it is?"

Sage groaned. "Oh, Mariah, don't tell me you're really falling for the guy? I mean, I know I've always wanted you to find somebody and I've been teasing you a bit about him. But seriously he's—well, he's one of Aimee's castoffs! You can't be getting serious thoughts about the man!"

Mariah's fingers unconsciously touched her fingers to the cross dangling against her throat. Aimee had already ruined one relationship for Mariah. She couldn't let her sister's memory interfere with her feelings for Finn. If she did, she'd be letting Aimee win a second time.

With her foot on the brake, Mariah pulled the gearshift into Drive. "I have to go," she said curtly. "I'll see you tomorrow."

Reaching a hand through the window, Sage squeezed Mariah's shoulder. "I'm sorry, Mariah. I shouldn't have said that. It was an awful thing to say. Finn is your business, not mine."

"Forget it," Mariah muttered. "I'll see you tomorrow."

She gave the other woman a halfhearted wave and quickly drove away.

At the same time on Stallion Canyon, Finn was working in the meadow, attaching a huge pipe to the irrigation pump, when his cell phone rang. Tossing the heavy wrench aside, he reached for the phone and was somewhat surprised to hear his father's voice on the other end of the connection.

"Did I catch you at a bad time?" Orin asked.

Still working to catch his breath, Finn said, "No. Just doing a bit of plumbing on an irrigation system. I think I'm close to having it going again."

"Irrigation system? Finn, what in hell is going on up there? I thought this trip was all about a baby."

Finn wiped a hand across his sweaty brow. "It is about Harry. But I can't just sit idle while we're waiting on the DNA results to come back. There's plenty of work to be done around here."

Orin spluttered. "There's a hell of a lot of work to do here on the Horn, too. Your home, remember?"

The testiness in Orin's voice put a grimace on Finn's face. "Yes, Dad. I remember. Is anything wrong there?"

Orin sighed. "No. I was calling just to check on you. I didn't mean to go off like that. It's just been—well, different with you away this long, Finn. I miss you. I want you to hurry up and get back here."

Finn leaned his back against the wheel on the irrigation line as warring emotions tore through him. From the time he was born, the Silver Horn had been his home, and he loved his family with every fiber of his being. But now there were new feelings growing inside him. For Harry and Mariah. And for Stallion Canyon. In spite of his ties back in Nevada, and in spite of the uncertainty of the future, he felt his roots sinking into this fertile land.

"Well, I've missed seeing everyone there. How are the horses? Any problems?"

"Not really. We've bred the last two mares. So the spring breeding is all wrapped up. Dandi, the yearling with the curly mane, cut her foot. We're not sure how. But Doc Pheeters has sewn it and seems to think it won't be a problem. Other than a scar."

"That's good." Finn's gaze wandered over the meadow. With the pump going, he could irrigate until the grass was growing thick and lush. The mustangs would thrive here. If only he had more time. But he expected that one day next week the DNA test would arrive in the mail. And then Mariah would be out of school and he'd have no reason to linger here on Stallion Canyon. Unless she asked him to stay. "Uh—did Clancy speak with you about the mustangs?"

There was a long pause. "No. What are you talking about?"

Damn it, he should have known Clancy wouldn't say

anything to their father about the mustangs. His brother didn't want to hear Orin yell any more than Finn did.

"I purchased ten mustangs from Mariah. They were the last ones she had here on the ranch. Five mares, four geldings and one stallion. A few nights ago, one of the mares foaled a filly, so I actually have eleven now. The baby is precious, Dad. She's bright chestnut with four white feet and a snip on her nose. She's going to be a real looker. And the other four mares will be delivering soon."

The pride that Finn was feeling was quickly smashed as Orin muttered several curse words. And for a split second Finn considered ending the call. But this was his father, and sooner or later he was going to have to deal with the situation. Might as well be now rather than later, he decided.

"What are you thinking, Finn? You know you can't put them on the Horn! Hell, your grandfather is probably going to have a stroke when he hears about this."

Angry and hurt, Finn pushed away from the irrigation wheel to stare across the sea of grass where spots of river glittered through the limbs like diamonds hanging from a Christmas tree.

"Then don't tell him!" Finn said tightly. "Because neither of you have anything to worry about. I damn well don't plan on bringing them to the Horn!"

"Then what are you planning to do?" Orin demanded.

"I haven't decided yet. But you can be sure of one thing. Wherever the mustangs go, I'll go with them! Now I have to go. Good-bye, Dad."

"Finn! Listen to me! I—"

Finn ended the connection and drew in several deep breaths in hopes it would cool his boiling blood. He'd probably just burned a bunch of bridges with that last shot he'd flung at his father, but Finn wasn't going to regret it. It was high time that his family realized he was a thirty-two-year-old man with dreams and desires of his own. He couldn't live his life according to a Calhoun edict.

That night as Mariah and Finn sat at the dinner table, she worriedly watched as he pushed the food around on his plate. From the moment he walked into the house this evening, he'd seemed preoccupied. Now as her gaze slid over his rugged features, she could see lines of fatigue around his eyes and mouth. But she had a feeling it wasn't fatigue that was making him withdrawn. Something else was wrong.

"If you don't care for the pork chops, Finn, I'll be happy to fix you something else."

His expression rueful, he glanced across the table at her. "I'm sorry, Mariah. The food is delicious. You've cooked everything just right."

To prove his point, he shoveled up a forkful of mashed potatoes and gravy and lifted it to his mouth.

She reached for her iced tea and took a long sip before she casually asked, "How's baby Poppy?"

A halfhearted grin crossed his face and the weak reaction told Mariah that something was definitely wrong. Normally, the mere mention of the newborn filly would light up Finn's whole demeanor. Tonight there was a sadness dimming his eyes and the sight troubled her greatly.

"She's getting spunkier every day. I might turn them into the meadow with the geldings tomorrow and give the baby a chance to stretch her legs."

"What about the mares?" Mariah asked, as she offered Harry a spoonful of pureed fruit.

"I'm happy with how they're looking. The brown mare's milk bag is getting full so I expect her to deliver in the next day or two."

Harry smacked his hands on the high chair tray and opened his mouth for another bite. As Mariah continued to feed the baby, she said, "I hope all the babies are born before it's time for you to ship them back to Nevada."

The silence that followed her comment had her looking over to see him staring moodily toward the windows behind her shoulder. Mariah decided it wasn't the time to prod him with questions. At best, her time with Finn was limited; she didn't want to waste it by picking and prodding at him.

After a moment, his gaze snapped back to hers and though he attempted to smile, she could see his heart was hardly in it. "Yes, I hope it will work out that way, too."

The remainder of the meal passed with Finn saying very little and Mariah focusing on feeding Harry the last of his food. Afterward, Finn helped her with the dishes, then excused himself to attend to chores at the barn.

While he was out of the house, Mariah readied Harry for bed, then graded a stack of test papers. She'd just finished the schoolwork and was carrying Harry toward the nursery when she heard Finn enter the house through the back door.

Changing directions, she met him in the breezeway. "I was on my way to the nursery to change Harry's diaper," she told him. "Was everything all right at the barn?"

An annoyed frown put a crease between his brows. "Everything was fine. Why do you keep asking me?"

Losing her patience, she snapped, "Maybe because

you're acting like you've lost your best friend. And you won't tell me what's wrong."

Not waiting on his reply, she turned and walked straight to the nursery. She'd laid Harry on the dressing table and was in the process of unsnapping the legs of his pants when she heard Finn's boots tapping against the tiled floor of the nursery.

"Let me do that," he said softly as he brushed her hands out of the way.

Saying nothing, she stood to one side and watched him deftly deal with Harry's soiled diaper, all the while talking to the boy in a hushed, gentle voice. When he had Harry dressed again, he positioned him over his shoulder, then turned toward Mariah.

"I'm sorry for snapping at you, Mariah." He blew out a heavy breath. "I have a lot on my mind—but that's no excuse."

Mariah had a lot on her mind, too. And all of it had to do with him and Harry. And where she might fit into their lives.

Placing her hand on his arm, she gave him a wobbly smile. "I'm sorry, too. Would you like to go sit on the back porch? I can make us some coffee if you'd like."

"Sounds nice. I'll take Harry with me," he told her.

A few minutes later, Mariah stepped onto the back porch, carrying a tray with the coffee and a few slices of pound cake. As she placed it on a small table, she looked over to see that Finn was sitting in the rocker with Harry already asleep in his arms.

He said, "Harry looked around for a minute or two and then his eyelids got droopy. I must be a dull daddy. Each time I hold him, he falls asleep."

Mariah smiled. "He feels contented and safe when you hold him. That's why he falls asleep."

"Well, now that you're here with the coffee, I'll put him in his playpen."

He carried Harry over to the playpen and covered him with a quilt to protect him from the cool evening air. Once he'd resumed his seat in the rocker, Mariah served him the coffee and cake, then sank into the chair angled to his left arm.

As she helped herself to a cup, he said, "I finished working on the irrigation pump this afternoon. So far it's working as it should."

"That's great. You must be a regular handyman. Dad always called a repairman out whenever it went on the blink."

He shrugged. "Dad made us boys learn to do other chores besides ride horses and chase cows. He always reminded us that ranching was much more than taking care of livestock."

"Sounds like your father is a wise man."

He turned a thoughtful gaze toward the mountain ridge to the east as he sipped at the coffee. "I used to think he could do no wrong. And I still love and respect him. But—"

Mariah gripped the handle of her cup as she waited for him to continue. When he didn't she asked, "Has something happened with your family, Finn?"

The shake of his head was so negligible, she barely caught it.

"Not exactly. Dad called while I was out at the meadow working on the pump. I told him about buying the mustangs and he threw a little cussing fit."

Mariah's heart was suddenly aching for him. She

knew what it was like to feel unappreciated and misunderstood. And she didn't want that for Finn. She could see for herself that he was a hardworking, responsible man. He deserved his family's consideration.

"So what did you tell him?" Mariah asked.

She watched his jaw tighten and the corners of his mouth curve downward. Apparently, the conversation he'd had with his father was still making him angry. Which surprised her. Since Finn had come to the ranch, she hadn't ever seen him in this dark of a mood.

He said, "That I'd find some other place to put them. And wherever the mustangs go, that's where I'll go."

She drew in a sharp breath. "Oh, Finn. That was a pretty definitive thing to say, wasn't it?"

"Yeah. It was pretty final, all right. Especially considering that after I said it, I hung up the phone," he said flatly. "Now I have to decide what to do. About the horses and myself."

Leaning forward, she studied his profile in the waning twilight. "Finn, what is this going to mean? About Harry? And—"

"We're still waiting on the DNA," he interrupted.

"We both know that's just a formality."

He stared at her. "A formality? You insisted on it!"

Her gaze dropped sheepishly to her lap. "I know," she mumbled. "But I felt we both needed that certainty. And I guess a part of me was grasping at straws. Wanting a reason to keep Harry here longer. And wanting to keep you here longer, too."

"Oh, Mariah."

Suddenly he was on his feet, reaching for both her hands. With her heart beating wildly, she allowed him to draw her from the chair and fold her into his arms.

"I don't want you to worry about the test. About Harry or us. I just want you to touch me, love me and make me forget everything. Except this."

His mouth came down on hers and she melted against him as his lips promised a pleasure that only he could give her. And as her mouth accepted the thrust of his tongue, the doubts and fears that were racing through her mind only moments ago were suddenly wiped away with a sweeping flame of desire.

"Let's get Harry and go inside," he whispered.

She smiled against his lips. "It's pretty early to go to bed. Especially when I'm not a bit sleepy."

He chuckled. "It's going to be a long, long time before you get any sleep, my darling."

Chapter Ten

Nearly a week later, on late Thursday afternoon, Finn was in the mares' paddock, studying their condition and trying to determine how long it would be before the last three dropped their foals. Two days ago the brown mare had safely delivered a black colt, and Finn was thrilled to see he was thriving and already running and bucking alongside his mother.

To help him get an idea of their due dates, Mariah had searched through some of the last notes Aimee had recorded regarding the ranch's breeding schedule. The dates had given him a fairly close idea of when the mares would deliver, but sometimes they were as unpredictable as women. The last thing he wanted to do was put them on a horse van to travel several hours. But time was winding down and sooner rather than later, he was going to have to decide what to do with the mustangs.

You have a hell of a lot more than the mustangs to

worry about, Finn. Mariah has built herself a home smack in the middle of your heart. So what are you going to do about her?

The nagging voice in his head prompted Finn to walk over to the wooden fence and stare thoughtfully toward the house. Tomorrow was Mariah's last day at school. And they both expected Harry's DNA test to arrive at any time now. Once that happened there would be no reason for him to continue to stay here on Stallion Canyon. Unless Mariah asked him to. And so far that hadn't happened. But then Stallion Canyon wasn't going to be hers for much longer. She might feel it was pointless to ask him.

During the past week their relationship had grown even deeper. At least, it had felt that way to Finn. Each night she'd made love to him as though a lifetime of kissing him, holding him, would never be enough. Yet she'd never whispered a word to him about love, or forever, or the future. And now, as time was closing in, he was beginning to wonder if she'd become his bed partner only to ease her loneliness, not because she was falling in love with him.

Was that what he wanted? To hear Mariah say she loved him? Because he'd already fallen in love with her? For the past few days Finn had been in a perpetual wrestling match with those questions. Now he was beginning to realize it had been wrong of him to expect Mariah to open her heart to him first. Especially when he'd not said a word to her about love or marriage, something he should've done days ago. But he'd hesitated because he'd wanted to make sure what he was feeling was more than infatuation or lust.

Finn had never been in love before. As a very young

man, he'd thought the attachment he'd felt to Janelle was love, but now he could see his relationship with her had been little more than a childhood crush that had lasted longer than it should have. What he felt for Mariah was much, much deeper. He wanted the connection they'd built between them to go on forever. If that was love, then he needed to decide what it meant for both of their futures.

Thoughts about Mariah were continuing to roll through his head when he suddenly spotted a man and woman he'd never seen before step out the back door of the house. Dressed in dark office-type clothing, the woman had short gray hair and was carrying some sort of briefcase beneath one arm. The man was tall and wearing traditional ranch clothing. From this distance, Finn guessed him to be somewhere in his fifties.

The two paused on the edge of the patio, then the woman pointed toward the barn. At that moment, Finn realized the woman had to be the real estate agent Mariah had hired to sell Stallion Canyon. Obviously, the man with her was a serious buyer. Otherwise, the woman would've never bothered to bring him all the way out here to view the property.

With a sick feeling swimming in the pit of his stomach, Finn let himself out of the paddock and walked over to the shed row. By then the man and woman were fast approaching, and not wanting to appear evasive or rude, he forced himself to stand there and wait for them to arrive.

The woman introduced herself to Finn as Ella Clark, a real estate agent from Alturas. The man with her was Don Larson, a rancher looking for a larger spread to run cattle. After a short exchange of small talk, Finn decided

Larson appeared friendly enough. But all the while the other man was talking, Finn was trying to picture him working around these barns and arena, of him living in the house and perhaps even sleeping in the same room where he and Mariah made love. The idea sickened Finn more than he'd ever imagined it would. It also made him realize just how much he'd come to think of Stallion Canyon as his home.

Smiling at Finn, Ella said, "Mr. Larson is looking for good grazing land. I've been telling him how the Montgomery family has raised horses on this land for years, so it's bound to have a good supply of grass."

"It's like any place else. It has to rain to have grass," Finn said bluntly.

The woman's brows shot up, while Larson asked, "And how often does it rain around here?"

"I'm not the one to ask. I'm just a temporary resident." The admission was worse than coughing up nails, Finn thought. But the truth just the same.

"Oh," the man said. "I thought you worked here."

Finn grimaced. "There are no hired hands here on Stallion Canyon. And pretty soon there won't be any horses."

Ella Clark awkwardly cleared her throat. "Things must've changed around here."

"Yeah. You could say that," Finn replied. "Now if you'll excuse me, I'll let you show Mr. Larson the rest of the property."

Finn quickly left the two of them and headed to the house. When he let himself into the kitchen, he found Linda sitting at the breakfast bar, sniffing back tears. Across the room, Harry was sitting in his high chair working diligently to eat a graham cracker.

"What's the matter?" he asked Linda.

She used the corner of a paper towel to dab her eyes. "To have people traipsing through here like—this place already belongs to someone else." She sucked in a deep breath and looked at him. "When I think of Ray I can hardly bear it."

Since Finn had gotten to know Linda, he was beginning to understand more and more that the woman had been very close to Mariah's father. And that fact was even more apparent as he watched tears roll down her face.

"I met them out at the barn," was all he could say. "He's only looking. It's hardly a done deal."

"If he doesn't buy, the next one will," she said bitterly, then turned her back to him.

There wasn't much Finn could say to that. Instead of trying, he walked over and plucked Harry out of the high chair. Holding the boy in his arms always comforted him. But this evening he could only think of how much his son was about to lose.

A short while later, at the end of the long gravel drive leading to the ranch house, Mariah stopped her car at a rural mailbox fastened to a fat fence post. She'd lowered the window on the driver's side and was plucking a stack of envelopes from the metal box when the sound of an approaching vehicle had her peering through the windshield.

She recognized Linda's old red Ford heading toward her, and from the wake of dust billowing behind it, the woman was in a hurry. Apparently she'd gotten Finn to watch Harry so she could leave early.

By the time Mariah closed the mailbox and tossed the correspondence in the passenger seat, Linda's vehicle was drawing near. Mariah lowered the passenger window and waited for Linda to stop alongside the car to give her some sort of explanation as to why she was leaving early. Instead, the truck sped on, even as Mariah waved at the woman.

Puzzled by Linda's unusual behavior, Mariah started to drive on, but a piece of mail suddenly caught her eye. With her foot back on the brake, she twisted her head to read the return address.

The word *Laboratory* was all she needed to see. The results of Harry and Finn's DNA test had finally arrived. One way or the other, they were about to find out whether Finn had a legal right to the boy, or if the search for Harry's real father was just now beginning.

With Linda's unusual behavior momentarily pushed to the back of her mind, Mariah finished the short drive to the ranch house and hurried inside through the back entrance.

Immediately she spotted Finn standing in front of the microwave. Harry was propped against his shoulder and at the moment was emitting hungry wails around the tiny fist crammed in his mouth.

"Hi, darlin'," he greeted. "I'm heating Harry a bottle. Linda's already gone. Maybe you saw her."

Mariah walked to the breakfast bar and placed the stack of mail on one end. "All I saw was a blur. She was flooring that old Ford. She must've been running late to an appointment in town."

The microwave dinged and Finn pulled out the warmed bottle. "No appointment. She was upset. I suggested she go on home and let me handle Harry."

"Upset?" Mariah frowned. "Linda is always a rock. Did she get bad news or something?"

Finn carried Harry over to the bar, and after he'd taken a seat on one of the stools, offered the baby his bottle. With Harry happily drinking, Finn looked up at Mariah and she couldn't help but notice that the usual sparkle in his blue eyes was definitely missing.

He said, "She considered it bad news. The real estate agent and a potential buyer just left the place a few minutes ago. Linda is pretty torn up that the ranch might be selling soon."

A heavy weight of doom fell on Mariah's shoulders and sank to the bottom of her stomach. "Ms. Clark called me earlier today and informed me she'd be showing the place today. I could hardly tell her that now wasn't a good time. No time would be a good time."

"Really?"

A month ago she would've been shouting hallelujah at the idea of the ranch being taken off her hands. Now the whole idea made her sick. Was that what being in love did to a woman? she wondered. Was that the reason she was looking at everything differently? This place had once seemed such a burden. Now it felt like a home again. And all because of Finn. But he would be going back to Nevada soon. It would be irresponsible of her to dream the foolish dream of keeping him and Harry here, wouldn't it?

Her throat suddenly aching, she said, "I've come to realize how much I still love this place, Finn. But I... Well, we'll talk about Stallion Canyon later. Right now, there's something more important."

She picked up the piece of mail and with a trembling hand, thrust it at him. "The results are here. I think you should be the one to open it. This is all about you and Harry."

His gaze gently probed hers. "It's all about you, too," he said quietly.

Tears stung the back of her eyes and in a hoarse voice, she said, "Please open the damned thing before I decide to set a match to it."

With one hand occupied with holding Harry's bottle, he used the other to lift the envelope to his mouth. Using his teeth, he tore off the end, then fished out the contents.

As he began to read, Mariah suddenly found herself standing next to his shoulder. And in spite of all the certainty she'd felt about Finn being Harry's father, her heart was pounding and her mouth had gone dry with fear. What if the DNA didn't match? Finn would be crushed. And so would she.

Eons seemed to drag by before he finally spoke, and by then Mariah's emotions had run the gamut from panic to joy and everything in between.

"I am Harry's father," he said simply.

Mariah began to tremble all over and she wasn't sure if the reaction was from relief or the realization that everything was suddenly coming to an end. Harry was truly Finn's child. And even though he'd asked her to travel with him to his family ranch in Nevada, the short stay there to help get Harry accustomed to new surroundings would be only a temporary bandage on the gaping wound in her heart.

Her hand came to rest on Finn's shoulder and as she looked down at Harry's cheek pressed against his father's strong chest, she could only feel a sense of rightness. Harry would always be loved. And dear God, that was the thing she wanted most for him.

"Are you happy?"

He looked up at her and she was relieved to see that the sparkle had returned to his eyes.

"In my heart Harry was already mine. But it's great to see it verified. How do you feel about the news?"

Her fingers squeezed his shoulder. "I wouldn't have wanted anyone but you to be Harry's father. That's the way I feel."

A slow grin lifted the corner of his mouth. "When Harry gets finished with this bottle, I'm going to kiss you."

Chuckling now, she bent and kissed him gently on the cheek. "I'm going to remind you of that."

That night after dinner, as Finn helped Mariah clear away the remnants of their meal, she had little to say and he could see that her thoughts were preoccupied with something. Now that the matter of the DNA test was resolved and her job was finished for the summer, she had to be wondering what was next for the three of them.

Finn realized she deserved to know his feelings and what his plans included. But how could he explain to her that everything inside him was scattered and racing in all different directions? The plans he'd had when he'd first arrived on Stallion Canyon no longer appealed to him. Now when he thought of his and Harry's future, Mariah had to be in it. But was that what she wanted too?

"Have you called your family to let them know about the DNA?"

Her question interrupted his thoughts and he glanced over to see her scraping scraps of leftover food into the garbage container.

Running a hand through his hair, he said, "No. What with feeding the horses and having dinner, I haven't had a quiet moment yet."

"Then go on and make your call," she urged him. "I'll finish things here."

He hesitated. "There's no hurry about it."

Placing the plate in the bottom of the sink, she turned to him. A puzzled frown creased her forehead. "Finn, if I didn't know better, I'd think you're putting off talking to your family."

Realizing he looked more than sheepish, he wiped a hand over his face. "To tell you the truth, I'm not looking forward to it."

Her brows pulled together. "But why? I thought you were thrilled about the test results."

"I am. But they'll be asking me questions that— Well, after the awful conversation I had with Dad, I'm not sure what I want to tell them—about anything."

"If you feel awkward about calling your father, then talk to one of your brothers," she suggested.

Yes, he could speak with Rafe. Of all his brothers he was closest to him. But even Rafe would want to know his plans, and Finn wasn't ready to give him, or anyone, answers. Not until he knew exactly how Mariah felt about him.

"I will, Mariah. Just give me time."

Her expression full of concern, she stepped closer and rested her palms against his chest. "Tell me what's bothering you, Finn. And don't give me the old 'everything is fine' routine. I can see you're troubled."

He let out a heavy breath. "I'm not troubled. I'm thinking." Forcing a smile on his face, he looped his arms around her in a loose embrace. "I haven't even congratulated you for finishing the school year. Are you excited about summer vacation?"

She smiled gently up at him and Finn desperately

wanted to crush his mouth down on hers and carry her to the bedroom. To feel the need in her lips and the urgency of her hands moving over him would send all the anguish and worry from his mind. But Harry was still awake. And once Finn started making love to her, he didn't want anything to interrupt them.

"I always enjoy my time off in the summer. But come next fall I'll be anxious to get back in the classroom. Teaching is a part of me, I guess."

And her teaching job was here. She couldn't have made that any plainer, Finn thought.

"Hmm. Well, I never was a teacher's pet. But maybe there's hope for me yet." He kissed her gently in the middle of her forehead, then dropped his hold on her. "If you don't mind, Mariah, I think I'll go out to the barn for a while and check on the mares."

"I don't mind. Take your time."

He planted another kiss on the top of her head, then left the house with Mariah staring worriedly after him.

It was nearly dark by the time she heard Finn return to the house. As his boots echoed on the tiled floor of the breezeway, she carefully tucked a blanket around Harry's shoulders. The baby was growing every day. Before long he would be sitting alone and crawling. And then he would be walking and racing all over the place. But she wouldn't be chasing after him. Not unless some sort of miracle happened. And so far in her life, she hadn't experienced any of those.

She turned away from the crib and was stepping through the open doorway when she crashed head-on into Finn. His big hands grabbed her shoulders and steadied her.

"Mariah! I was just coming to see if you were here in the nursery. Did I hurt you?"

"No," she quickly assured him. "I heard you crossing the breezeway, but I thought you'd gone to your bedroom. Sorry I wasn't watching where I was walking."

His hands began to knead her shoulders. "Don't be sorry. I like being whammed in the belly by a beautiful brunette."

Beautiful. Not until Finn had come into her life had she ever felt truly beautiful. Oh, she'd been told in so many words by other men that she was attractive, but none of the compliments had come across as sincere. But something about the way Finn looked at her, touched her, made her feel special and womanly.

Laughing softly, she splayed her hands against his midsection. "I won't wham you again, but maybe I can think of doing something else you might like."

He pulled her close and whispered against her lips, "Is Harry asleep?"

"Yes." She slipped her arms around his waist. "How was everything at the barn? Did you have a good visit with the mares?"

"I'll tell you about it later," he said, then with a heady groan he closed the tiny space between their lips.

Minutes later, in the dusky dark interior of the bedroom, Mariah pushed everything from her mind except Finn. With his mouth fastened over hers and the thrusts of his hips driving into hers, thinking became impossible. Tiny bolts of lightning were exploding, creating a glorious network against the stormy swell of her emotions. Inside and out, from her head to her feet, every feminine cell in her body was glowing and aching for the man in her arms.

Pleasure was pouring through her and she wanted to give it all back to him. She wanted to thrill him more and more. She wanted to love him until their hearts had merged so tightly together that years of time could never untangle them.

Suddenly his mouth lifted from hers and his hoarse voice whispered against her cheek. "Oh, Mariah, Mariah—my sweet darling. I can't get enough of you."

"Love me, Finn," she breathlessly pleaded. "Keep on loving me."

With a needy groan, he rolled them over until his back was against the mattress and Mariah was riding the urgent thrusts of his hips. Gripping his shoulders, she hung on, matching his rhythm even though her lungs were burning, her heart pounding out of control. Like tangled threads, her body grew tighter and tighter until she was wrapped in captive knots.

She was crying his name, searching for relief, when he suddenly crushed her to him and buried his face in the side of her neck. In the next instant his warmth began to spill into her and suddenly she felt everything at once as sensations rocketed through her, blinding her with an ecstasy so great it momentarily stopped her breathing. And like a cornflower beneath a hot, hot sun, she bowed, then wilted completely.

It was long moments later before Mariah realized her cheek was resting against the sheet rather than the cool, grassy ground and the heat of the sun was actually the warmth of Finn's chest pressed against her back.

Turning into all that delicious warmth, she wrapped her arm around his waist and rested her head in the hollow of his shoulder.

With a contented groan, he lifted a hand to her hair and slowly stroked the thick strands lying against her back.

"Do you know how it makes me feel to have you here in my arms like this?" he asked.

His voice was still husky with desire, and the sound touched her as much as the calloused tips of his fingers. Both sent shivers of pleasure through her that knew no bounds.

"No," she whispered. "How does it make you feel?"

"Perfect. Absolutely perfect."

"Nothing is perfect," she said drowsily.

He chuckled softly. "You're wrong. I'm holding perfection in my arms."

Tilting her head back, she studied his face in the growing darkness. "You must have a bottle of wine or something hidden out at the horse barn. You're thinking is a little cockeyed."

Groaning, he pressed a kiss to her forehead. "My thinking has never been better."

"Really? This evening during dinner you seemed pretty mixed up about something."

His expression softened as his hand gently cupped the side of her face. "Hmm, I think I've been mixed up ever since I came to Stallion Canyon and laid eyes on you for the first time."

Her heart slowed as she anxiously tried to read the emotions on his face. There was a serious intensity in his eyes that she hadn't seen before. And she was suddenly afraid to guess what it might mean.

"That's understandable," she said. "Learning about Harry—that he was most likely your son, then coming up here to meet us—that had to be traumatic for you."

"I'm not talking about Harry now. I'm talking about you. And what you've done to me."

Lifting her hand, she pushed her fingers through the crisp burnished waves above his ear. "And what is that?" she asked softly.

Bending his head, he rubbed his cheek against her. "You've made me fall in love with you, my darling."

Mariah desperately needed to breathe, but her lungs seemed to have suddenly quit working.

"In love?" she whispered. "Is that what you just said?"

Drawing her closer, his hand made wide, sweeping circles across back. "That's exactly what I said. Why do you sound so surprised? Haven't I pretty much been saying that to you every night this past week or so?"

She'd wanted to believe the eagerness in his kisses and the urgency of his fiery touches were born from love. She'd even let herself imagine him saying those words to her. Yet she wasn't that same naive girl who'd once been duped by promises and pretty words. Once Aimee and Kris had betrayed her, she'd closed her heart to believing and hoping she would ever be truly loved.

Her throat suddenly tight, she said, "What you've been saying to me these past several nights is that you enjoy having sex with me. That's something very different than love."

He pulled back far enough to study her face. "I understand the difference, Mariah. And I can assure you that what I feel for you isn't just—raw desire. Yes, I want you. Yes, it's thrilling to have sex with you. But what I'm feeling goes way beyond that."

Not daring to believe the conviction in his voice, she sat up in the bed and drew the sheet over her breasts. "I don't know what to say, Finn. I wasn't expecting anything like this from you."

He scooted to a sitting position and once he was facing her, reached for her hand. As he wrapped his fingers around hers, she tried to still her racing mind, but it was impossible. What was the matter with her? Why couldn't she listen to her heart, wrap her arms around him and tell him that she loved him with every fiber of her being?

"Mariah, I've thought about this over and over. What I feel for you isn't going to end. And I—well, I don't want us to ever be apart. I realize that the first day I was here I asked you to go back to Nevada with me. But I don't want that now."

Trembling now, she stared at him. "You don't? But why? What—"

Before she could finish, he reached for her other hand and drew her closer. "I want us to be married, Mariah. I want the three of us to make our home here."

Her mouth fell open as she forced herself to breathe. Him and her and Harry together as a family. It would be a dream come true. If she could only believe that weeks and months from now, he'd still be wanting her. That she'd be enough woman to keep him happy.

"I think—you're getting way ahead of yourself. You haven't thought this through, Finn. Not completely."

"What have I not thought through? Marrying you?" he asked wryly. "Or making my home here?"

"Both. We haven't known each other that long and—"

"Long enough," he interrupted. "I've had plenty of time to realize how much I love you. And this evening, after I read the DNA letter, it dawned on me that everything was coming together. That I couldn't wait to tell you how I feel."

Her heart was aching to believe every word he was saying. For days now she'd been wondering how she could possibly go on living once he and Harry moved to Nevada. But she'd been too cautious for too long to simply let herself fall into his arms and promise to marry him. She'd done that once before and ended up getting her heart stomped. But this time there was more than the risk of breaking her heart. Harry's welfare had to be considered, too.

"Finn, you're suffering a memory lapse. This ranch is up for sale. You just saw Mr. Larson looking things over this afternoon. He could decide at any moment to put money down and—"

"I want you to contact Ella Clark in the morning and tell her that you've changed your mind and you're not going to sell Stallion Canyon."

The shock of his words actually caused her to rear back. "Not sell? Finn, the ranch is going under!"

A patient smile curved the corners of his mouth. "Only because it needs someone with money and the experience to run it. I certainly fall into both those categories."

"But why? You already have a prestigious job—a fancy home back in Nevada. Your family and friends are there and—"

"But I want you to be my family, Mariah. You and Harry. The three of us here on Stallion Canyon. You've already said that Harry should eventually inherit this ranch. I can make that possible. Even though willing it to Harry might prove to be a problem later on," he added with a sly grin.

"What do you mean?"

"Our other children might feel like they deserve a part of the ranch, too."

Other children? Oh God, he was going too fast for her. She couldn't think beyond this moment. She hadn't yet been able to completely grasp the notion that he could possibly love her and want to marry her.

"So what about your family? Your work on the Silver Horn? You can just turn your back on all that and stay here? That would be a huge change for you, Finn."

His hands closed firmly over her shoulders. "For a long time I've been thinking I could never be truly happy unless I branched out on my own. This argument I've had with my father and grandfather about the mustangs has been going on for a long while. Now I actually own some of them. And this is the perfect place to raise them, to do the kind of work I've always dreamed about doing. Can't you see, Mariah? Everything is just perfect. All you have to do is tell me that you love me. That you want to marry me."

Perfect. Yes, she thought sickly. It was all too perfect. He couldn't take his mustangs home to the Silver Horn, so he'd decided that keeping them here and using this ranch for his personal plans would be far more convenient.

"I'm sorry, Finn. I can't."

Tears were already gathering at the back of her eyes as she quickly scooted away from him and swung her legs over the side of the bed.

She was pulling on her robe when she heard Finn leave the bed, then the faint rustle of clothing. The next instant, he was standing in front of her, wearing nothing but jeans and a deep frown on his face. And as Mariah's gaze wandered over his perfectly carved torso and the thick hank of hair falling over his blue eye, she wondered if she'd lost her mind.

To have this man as her husband, under any circumstances, would be enough to make most any woman happy. But for as long as she could remember, she'd settled for less. Aimee had been the one who'd been loved and adored by every male who'd gotten within speaking distance of the two sisters. While Mariah had been grateful for any crumbs of affection that were left over. But she was finished with being grateful. Of selling herself short.

"Can you give me one good reason?" he asked gruffly.

Lifting her chin, her gaze defiantly met his. "I want a man to marry me because he loves me. Not because it's convenient. Or gives him everything he wants in one neat little package. No thanks, Finn."

"Then you're turning me down flat?"

He sounded incredulous, and anger spurted through her. No doubt he'd figured she was so weak-minded and besotted with him that the idea of her refusing his proposal had never entered his mind.

"Not only am I turning you down, but I think you need to start making plans to leave here. The sooner, the better!"

A muscle jumped in his jaw and for a split second, Mariah would've sworn she saw pain shadow his eyes. But as he silently turned and left the room, she couldn't be sure about anything, except that her heart had just splintered into a pile of painful pieces.

Chapter Eleven

The next morning Finn made sure he was out of the house before Mariah appeared in the kitchen for coffee. It would've been unbearable to sit across from her at the breakfast table, sharing a morning meal as though they were still a couple.

A couple. Had they ever been truly that? he wondered dismally. He'd thought so. Ever since that night the filly had been born and the two of them had first made love, he'd believed something rich and real had happened between them. And last night, before he'd proposed her, he'd been sure he felt love in her kisses, heard it in her sighs.

But now she wanted him gone. She wanted nothing to do with marrying him. She refused to consider the three of them making a home on this beautiful ranch. Why had she twisted his hopes and dreams? His plans for their future together?

I want a man to marry me because he loves me. Not because it's convenient. Or gives him everything he wants in one neat little package.

In spite of the long, miserable hours that had passed since she'd said those words to him, they were still echoing through him, tormenting him with frustration.

Oh God, why would she think he was using her just to get a ranch? Hell, all it took to get a piece of land was money. And he had plenty of that. He'd have no problem acquiring land for his mustangs. But he couldn't come up with another woman. Not one that he loved to distraction. Not one that he wanted to be with until his life on this earth was over.

So what are you going to do now, Finn? She's ordered you to leave. Maybe you ought to head back to the house and put up a persuasive argument.

The cynical voice in his head had him groaning as he paused beneath the shed row. If he had to argue and plead to get a woman to marry him, then she clearly wasn't the wife he needed.

A black rubber feed bucket was sitting at the gate to one of the stalls. Finn flipped it over and once he'd taken a seat, pulled out his cell phone. At this hour of the morning, Sassy had more than likely fed the kids and headed out to the barn.

His sister answered on the second ring, and the sound of her cheerful voice caused his heart to wince. She was the one person who seemed to truly understand him.

"Finn, how did you guess I was just about to call you?"

"I have telepathy with my sister. But I can't guess what you were going to call me about. You sound happy about something."

"Oh, I am! And you're going to be the first to hear. After Jett, that is. I'm pregnant!"

Her announcement almost had him forgetting his own problems. But not quite. Just the mention of the word had him envisioning Mariah carrying his child.

"Pregnant? Again? Are you kidding me?"

Sassy laughed. "Why, no. Why do you sound so amazed? You knew that Jett and I wanted a big family. This one will only be number three."

"Well, yes, I was aware that you two wanted more kids, but little Skyler was only born a few months ago! Don't you need a rest?"

His question brought another crow of laughter from her. "Me rest? Finn, I'll do that when I get old. Besides, Gypsy is a wonderful nanny. When I'm out working with the cattle or horses, I don't have to worry one second about the kids. I know she's taking care of everything."

Yes, Sassy had been lucky in finding the young Shoshone woman to care for her children. If only he could be that lucky in finding a nanny for Harry, Finn thought. Because it was quite obvious that Mariah wasn't going to be around to make sure his son had the care he needed.

"Well, if you and Jett are happy about the coming baby, then I'm thrilled, too."

"Awww, thanks, dear brother, I knew you'd be happy for me," she said with affection, then swiftly changed the subject. "So what were you calling about? You got news about the DNA?"

Oh Lord, it seemed like it had been days ago since he'd opened that letter, instead of last night. So much had happened that his head was still spinning. And his heart—well, the pain it was causing him was so excruciating it was indescribable.

"Last evening. I'm Harry's father, all right."

"Oh, Finn. That's wonderful. Are you happy about it?"

"I'm happy and relieved. I think I loved him from the moment I held him in my arms." He took a deep breath and let it out. "So we'll be coming home—probably tomorrow. That's why I'm calling. I need your help."

"Sure. Anything."

He looked over at the mares milling about in the paddock. The two that had already foaled were now out to pasture with their babies. The other three he'd kept confined so that he could keep a close watch on their progress.

"I've bought ten mustangs plus two new babies and I need to find a place to put them for a while. Until I can come up with a permanent spot to keep them. I thought—maybe you had a few acres I could use. That land on the north edge of your ranch is still empty, isn't it?"

"Yes, but there's no water there yet. Unless it rains. And God only knows when that might happen. But forget about that. You can use the section on the west side of the ranch. We don't have any cattle on it right now. And the windmill is in good working order. You might have to feed them a bit, but I think they'll find a little to graze on."

"But you might need that pasture soon, Sassy. Jett might not like the idea of me using it."

She laughed as though his suggestion was ludicrous. "I run the ranch. Jett runs his law office. Whatever decisions I make about the livestock or land are fine with him. Besides, he loves you. He'll be glad we could help."

Finn swallowed at the lump that had suddenly formed

in his throat. "Thanks, Sassy. I really appreciate it. What with Dad and Gramps—"

"You don't have to explain, Finn. You and I have talked about this before. Frankly, I'm really happy that you've taken this step. It's something you've always wanted to do. And you're going to do great with the mustangs. I just know it."

"Hearing you say that means a lot to me. Especially—"

He broke off as his gaze strayed toward the house. Now wasn't the time to explain his broken relationship with Mariah. Maybe later after he'd gotten back to Nevada, he could talk to Sassy about it.

"Especially, what?" she prompted when he didn't go on. "Is anything wrong, Finn? You don't exactly sound like yourself."

"I'm fine. What with getting Harry ready to go and making arrangements for the horses to be shipped, I have a lot to deal with."

"Dealing with a thousand things at once has always been easy for you, Finn. And you do it with a happy grin. But you don't sound exactly happy to me right now. Having a new son without any time to prepare to become a dad would be pretty overwhelming. If you need me to help, Finn, just tell me. Gypsy can handle one more baby…if you'd like to come stay with us for a while."

"Thanks, but no. I— My job is waiting on me at the ranch. And the sooner I get Harry settled in there, the better off we'll both be," he said flatly. "But there is something else you can do for me."

"Name it."

"Call Rafe and tell him I'll be heading home tomorrow. He can let the others know."

"Oh, you don't want to speak with your brother?" she asked thoughtfully.

"No."

There was a long pause and then she said, "Okay. I love you, Finn. See you when you get home."

"I love you, too, sis," he told her, then ended the call before she could guess the gruffness in his voice was actually the sound of his broken heart.

Later that morning, Mariah was in her father's old room, sitting at a desk where she kept all the ranch's paperwork. The bills stacked in front of her were enough to make her sick to her stomach. But her worry over the unpaid bills was minor compared to the misery she felt over Finn.

You brought it all on yourself. Instead of telling him you love him and want to marry him, you had to get all indignant and start accusing him of wanting this ranch more than he wants you. I hope your pride is worth this, Mariah.

Bending her head, she pressed fingertips to her closed eyelids and willed the mocking voice in her head to go away. She felt bad enough without it constantly reminding her that she'd ruined everything between them. As if anyone could ruin a fairy tale, she thought bitterly. Because that's all it had been. Just wishful dreaming on her part.

A light knock on the door brought her head up and she glanced around to see Finn standing in the open doorway. The sight of him caused everything inside her to go rigid with pain.

"Sorry to interrupt," he said flatly. "But there are a few things I need to discuss with you."

She rose to her feet. "We had our discussion last night," she said hoarsely. "There's nothing more to be said."

He walked into the room. "I'm not here to discuss any of that. We both said enough on the subject last night. I'm here to talk about Harry. I've informed my family that I'll be heading home tomorrow. Can you have his things ready to go by midmorning?"

If she hadn't been holding on to the back of her chair, Mariah felt sure she would have wilted to the floor. Her knees felt like wet sponges and her heart was beating a loud protest against her ribs.

"Yes. I'll have everything packed."

"Good. A livestock transporter will be here early in the morning to pick up the mustangs. So I plan to leave shortly after the horses do."

Tomorrow. He and Harry would be leaving tomorrow. She'd told him that the quicker he left, the better. He was giving her just what she'd asked for. The reality of it left her numb.

"What about the mares? Aren't you worried one of them might go into labor during the trip?"

His expression turned harder than granite. "You're not worried. Why should I be?"

She supposed she deserved that. But he ought to understand that the longer he remained here, the more difficult it would be for everyone.

"I wouldn't mind if you left them," she offered stiffly. "At least until they've foaled."

"No thanks. I want them with me."

So he'd already found a place to put the mustangs, she thought. She wanted to ask him where they'd be going, but if he'd wanted her to know that, he would have told her. Besides, the mustangs were no longer her worry. After tomorrow horses would never be a part of her life. Neither would Finn. As for Harry, an occasional visit with her little nephew would be the most she could hope for.

"I see. Well, I'll start getting Harry's things collected and packed. Do you think—uh, you can make the trip okay with him? I mean, traveling with a baby isn't easy."

He stared at her, his expression unflinching. "We'll make it fine," he said flatly. "Without you."

Tears burned her throat as she walked over to stand in front of him. "I'm sorry, Finn. That—things didn't work out."

"I'm sorry, too, Mariah. Damned sorry."

He turned and left the room and as Mariah watched him go, she had to fight the urge to run after him. He and Harry were everything to her. She didn't want them to go. But on the other hand, she wanted to be loved just for being her. Not because she owned a ranch or was a ready-made mother.

Maybe that kind of love would never come to her. But she had to hope and believe that someday it would.

An hour later, Mariah was in the nursery, packing Harry's toys into a cardboard box while on the other side of the room, Linda sat rocking Harry.

"Have you lost your mind, Mariah?"

Mariah frowned at the woman. "I feel very sane at the moment, thank you."

"Yeah, but how will you feel tomorrow? How will you feel when you see Harry and Finn drive away?"

Mariah's jaw tightened as she tried to steel herself against that heartbreaking image. "I'll feel like my life is taking on a new beginning."

"Like hell," Linda muttered. "You're going to be

crushed. You're going to realize what a mistake you're making."

The only mistake she'd made was in thinking Finn had taken her to bed because he really loved her. When all along, his main thoughts had been on this ranch and making it a home for a herd of mustangs.

Dear Lord, he'd turned out to be more like her father than she could've ever imagined. Her daddy had been a man who'd worn spurs and now Harry's daddy wore them, too. She supposed that was fitting. At least Aimee would've been happy about it. But for the past few days, Mariah had felt as though she'd truly become important to Finn. Much more important than a herd of mustangs and a piece of land.

"Linda, when Finn told me he loved me, I would have believed him—if he'd stopped right there. But in the next breath, he was saying he wanted this ranch and how perfect it would be for his mustangs. What am I supposed to think—feel?"

Linda's short laugh was mocking. "Mariah, listen to yourself. What do you think this ranch has been for the past twenty years? Your father put his heart and soul into this land to make it a great place to raise horses. You should be proud and happy that Finn can appreciate that."

Mariah picked up a little brown teddy bear with intentions of placing it in the box, but somehow it found its way to her chest, where she pressed it tight against her aching heart. "I don't have to tell you what it was like for me...with Dad. And Aimee. Stallion Canyon was their life, their love. I was just around. And then when things went wrong with Kris..." As her words trailed away, she shook her head. "It doesn't matter anymore. None of it matters."

Harry let out another fussy cry and Linda rose from the rocker and began to bounce the baby in her arms. "Is that why you don't care whether Finn takes Harry out of your life? Because he's actually Aimee's baby? Because Finn made love to Aimee before he made love to you?"

Whirling around, Mariah glared at her. "That's a low blow."

"I meant for it to be," she said sharply, then started toward the door. "I'll be in the kitchen putting some ice on Harry's gums."

Once Linda and Harry had disappeared, Mariah covered her face with both hands and sucked in several long breaths in an attempt to collect herself. But her effort did little to compose her ragged emotions. With a watery wall of tears blurring her vision, she finished packing Harry's things.

Two weeks later, Finn was sitting in his office, a small square room located inside the main horse barn on the Silver Horn Ranch. For the past hour he'd been staring at a catalog for an upcoming horse auction, trying to determine if any of the offered horses were something the Horn could use, but his heart wasn't in the effort.

Finally, he tossed aside the catalog and was scanning through the newspaper when his father knocked on the open door and stepped into the room.

At sixty-three, Orin Calhoun was still an imposing figure of a man. Tall and broad-shouldered, with thick iron-gray hair that waved away from his face, he was in top physical shape. He could outride and out-rope most of the hands on the Silver Horn, and he didn't let them forget it, either.

"Am I interrupting?" Orin asked.

Finn folded the newspaper and placed it to one side of the desktop. "Not at all. Just catching up on the news."

Orin sank into one of the straight-backed chairs sitting at an angle to Finn's messy desk. He cocked a brow at the newspaper, then looked directly at his son. "I didn't realize they printed news articles in the classifieds. I'll have to start reading that section of the paper, too. Just to make sure I don't miss anything," he said pointedly.

Finn bit back a sigh. Even though Orin had happily welcomed Finn back home, the strained words they'd exchanged over the mustangs were still standing between them. Once he'd informed his father that Sassy had given the horses a temporary home, Orin had dropped the subject completely. Even so, Finn wasn't fooled by the silence. Orin and his grandfather Bart were silently keeping an eye on anything and everything Finn had been doing since he returned from Stallion Canyon. And the notion irked him greatly.

"Actually, I was going through the real estate ads to see if there was any land I might be interested in buying."

Orin grimaced. "We have all the land we need here on the Silver Horn."

"It's not mine. It belongs to the family."

"And you're a part of this family, Finn. For a while there I was thinking you'd forgotten that. But now you're home and hopefully getting settled back in your old routine."

Two weeks. That's how much time had actually passed since Finn had driven away from Stallion Canyon. But it felt more like two hundred weeks since he'd last seen Mariah's lovely face.

There'd been a flood of tears in her eyes when she'd said good-bye to Harry that morning on the front porch of the ranch house. But she'd said nothing to Finn. In fact, she hadn't even looked at him. She'd walked back into the house and left him standing there like a hopeful fool.

Since then, Harry was slowly getting accustomed to his new surroundings, but he was clearly still missing Mariah. There'd been times these past couple of weeks when he'd cried for no reason and nothing seemed to make him happy. During those times the women of the house had tried their best to pacify him, but Harry wanted Mariah. He wanted his mother—the one thing Finn couldn't give him.

So far he hadn't attempted to hire a nanny. What with Lilly already being in the house watching over her two children, and Tessa, the young ranch-house maid, to help with Harry, the two women kept insisting he didn't need a nanny. And frankly, Finn was loath to start interviewing women for the position.

All along, he'd planned on Mariah being with him and the two of them caring for their son together. Now that those plans had been crushed, he didn't know where to begin or how to start feeling like a human being again, instead of a miserable fool.

"Things with the horses are slow now that foaling season is over," Finn replied.

"There's plenty of training for you to oversee," Orin told him. "And Dad and I have been talking about purchasing a new stallion for the ranch's working remuda. Blue Cat is getting on in years. We need to bring another stallion in before his fertility drops. And we'd like to hear your input on the bloodlines you think would fit."

Rimrock. He was the sturdy stallion this ranch needed. But Finn would be wasting his breath to make such a suggestion. Instead, he bit back a weary sigh and said, "Sure. I'll think on the matter."

He felt his father's gaze boring into him.

"I've never heard you sound so enthusiastic."

"Sorry. I guess I haven't had time to get back into the swing of things yet."

"You don't need time to do a job you normally could manage with both eyes closed. Is this about Harry? Are you thinking that having a baby son has cramped your style?"

Incensed, Finn stared at his father. "My style! You make it sound like I'm some sort of playboy or something. Hell, just because I had one brief fling with a woman! Even before I met Aimee, I rarely left this ranch for any reason. And that includes spending time with the opposite sex. So, no! Harry hasn't cramped anything. I love him dearly."

"Then it's something else. You're moping about those damned mustangs, aren't you? You're still angry with me and your grandfather because we don't want any part of them. Well, if it means that much to you, then bring the things over here and put them out on the far west range. Just make sure the fence is bull strong."

Finn rose from his chair and walked over to the doorway. As he stared down the alleyway of the huge horse barn, he realized that he could look in any direction and see the best of everything. Horses, equipment, facilities, and competent ranch hands. Here Finn didn't have to want for anything. But as thankful as he was, it wasn't quite enough. And that realization only served to make him feel worse.

"Thanks, but that's not what I want."

Finn heard his father stir from the chair and then his strong hand closed over his shoulder.

"I'm sorry, Finn. That didn't sound very sincere. And I—well, I didn't come out here to fight with you about the mustangs. Far from it. I can see how miserable you've been and I don't want that. I want my son to be happy. To hell with what your grandfather wants. Bring the mustangs home. It'll be fine with me and him—once I set him straight."

But that was just it, Finn thought. Home didn't feel the same to him anymore. Home was back on Stallion Canyon with Mariah. Holding her, kissing her and making love to her. He'd thought it would never end. Their meals together and the precious playtime they'd shared with Harry. Those hours and days had been burned into his memory. He couldn't shake them. And today he'd reached the decision that he didn't want to shake them. He wanted them back. But how to manage that miracle was still something he hadn't figured out.

"I don't want that, Dad."

"Finn, I—"

"I'm not angry," Finn gently interrupted. "And I do appreciate the offer. But I want a place of my own." He turned to look at his father and was surprised to see a wry acceptance on his face. "You've told me that when my great-grandfather started the Silver Horn he didn't own much and this place was just a ragged piece of desert. But he had a dream, a plan. And he went for it. I don't think it's wrong for me to want the same things he wanted."

Orin patted his shoulder with understanding. "No, son. It's not wrong. I'd hoped the Horn would be your lifelong calling. But ever since you returned from California, it's become obvious to me that you need more to make you completely happy. And that's what I want for you, Finn, to be happy. Even if it means I have to give you a loose rein. Whatever it takes, I want you to go for it."

"Yeah," Finn said softly. "Whatever it takes."

The following week Mariah was sitting cross-legged in the middle of the floor of Aimee's old bedroom. Boxes of clothes, photos, horsemanship ribbons and trophies, and other souvenirs were scattered here and there, while a few books and stuffed animals were piled directly in front of her.

At the moment, Mariah's thoughts were lost in the past as she held a tiny gold locket in her palm. It was one of the last pieces of jewelry she'd seen her sister wear. At the time Mariah hadn't taken much notice of the necklace. Aimee had always had piles of inexpensive fashion jewelry lying around. But now as she opened up the little locket and found a tiny picture of Finn inside, an overwhelming sense of loss and bitterness swept over her. Maybe her sister had actually cared about Finn, she thought. In any case, he'd deeply affected both of their lives.

"Mariah? Are you home?"

The sudden sound of Linda's voice calling out to her had Mariah snapping the locket shut and dropping the piece into her shirt pocket. "In here, Linda. In Aimee's old room."

Moments later, the woman appeared in the open

doorway. "What a mess!" she exclaimed. "What are you doing dragging out all this stuff? Haven't you had enough to cry over here lately without getting into Aimee's things?"

Mariah sighed. "I've been putting off sorting through my sister's things, but I decided I can't keep doing that. Whenever I leave here and start living in an apartment I won't have room to keep Aimee's stuff. I'm going to pick out a few pieces to keep and give the rest to charity."

Linda entered the room and sank onto the edge of the queen-size bed. Mariah rose to her feet and dusted off the backside of her jeans.

"Sorry about the mess," Mariah told her. "Want to go to the kitchen for coffee?"

"In a bit." Gesturing toward the things on the floor, Linda asked, "So other than this project have you been keeping yourself occupied?"

Since Harry and Finn had left, she'd only seen her friend a couple of times. Once when Linda had attended graduation ceremonies at the high school where Mariah was employed. The second time had been about a week ago when the two women had inadvertently spotted each other in the produce section of a local supermarket.

"As best as I can now that school is out. And the house is—well, like a tomb with Harry not around. I can't even bear to walk into the nursery. It's still the same as it was the day that Finn and Harry left," she finished woefully. "What about you? How does it feel not to be a nanny to Harry anymore?"

Linda grimaced. "I hate it. Just like I hate the thought of you moving away from here. Have you heard more from that Clark woman? Is anyone getting closer to buying?"

Mariah shook her head. "No. As far as I know the man who came out for a look at the place has momentarily cooled his heels about buying. Ms. Clark keeps reminding me that the lending rules on mortgages are much stricter than they used to be. And the real estate market is still a little slow in our area. She tells me I need to be patient."

Linda let out a breath of relief. "Thank God! Maybe you'll come to your senses before a buyer shows up."

Groaning, Mariah picked up one of the boxes of clothing and sat it on the end of the bed. "Get real, Linda. Right now there's a stack of bills on the end of the bar just waiting to be mailed. But I can't do anything with them until my paycheck goes into the bank. And then hopefully there will be enough left over to buy groceries and gasoline for the car."

"Everyone has a sob story, Mariah. You think you have a corner on hard times?"

Linda's cutting remarks were so unlike her that Mariah was momentarily stunned. She dropped the sweater she'd plucked out of the box. "What in heck is wrong with you?"

Linda raised back up to a sitting position. "It disgusts me to see you losing everything that was ever important in your life, while you just stand around doing nothing about it."

Mariah walked around to the side of the bed and took a seat a short space from Linda. "What am I supposed to do about it? Harry is Finn's child, not mine. I had no right to keep him here."

"I wasn't just talking about Harry. But now that you've mentioned him, how is he? Has anyone been keeping you informed?"

"Not Finn, if that's what you're getting at," she said glumly. "His sister-in-law, Lilly, has been seeing after Harry and she's called me a few times. She says he's getting adjusted. And his tooth finally broke through. The first one. I kept hoping that would happen before he left. But—"

Her throat too choked to go on, she bent her head and tried to swallow away the burning pain.

"Here. None of that," Linda gently scolded. "Let's go to the kitchen. I'll make some coffee while you pull yourself together."

Out in the kitchen, Mariah took a seat at the bar and waited for Linda to brew the coffee. By the time the other woman joined her, Mariah was able to accept the cup of coffee and give her friend a lopsided smile.

"Thanks. And sorry about all the whining. I've been telling myself I'm not going to be doing any more of it, but—I'm still having my moments. And going through Aimee's things hasn't made matters any easier."

Linda sighed. "Aimee was irresponsible and most of the time I wanted to smack her and tell her to wake up. But I loved her. With everything inside me I wish she was still alive."

"I wish that same thing, too," Mariah murmured thoughtfully. "Except that—well, it would be hard for me to see her and Finn married and raising Harry together. That's awful of me, isn't it?"

Linda shook her head. "Trust me, Mariah, if your sister was still living she and Finn wouldn't be married. She was hardly his type."

"She must've been his type," Mariah argued. "They had a child together."

"It hardly takes a long-term relationship to make a

child. No, he would've figured Aimee out very quickly. Now you, Mariah, are a different matter. I saw the way Finn looked at you. I've never seen so much adoration in any man's eyes."

"I don't want to talk about Finn. It—hurts too much."

"Maybe you need to hurt. Long and hard. Maybe then you'll realize how wrong you were to send him away."

Confused, Mariah look at the older woman. "Why are you being so mean to me today?"

"I'm not being mean. I'm trying to wake you up— before it's too late."

Mariah stared at the brown liquid in her cup. "Oh, Linda, don't you think I've been asking myself over and over if I was wrong? If I should've trusted Finn completely? There are moments when I think I must have been crazy to send him away. And then others when I realize I was right to stand up for myself, my feelings. But even that doesn't make me feel any better now. Having Finn and Harry gone is making me ache all the way to my bones."

Linda placed her coffee cup on the bar, then turned to Mariah. "I think it's time I told you something. About your dad. And me."

Mariah's head came up. "What could Dad have to do with me and Finn? He's been gone for more than four years now."

"And I've grieved for the man every day of those years," Linda said bluntly.

Mariah continued to study the rueful expression on Linda's face. "I realize you loved him, too. Like a friend."

"No. That's where you're confused. I loved him like a woman loves a man. And Ray loved me. But all those years we could've been together—really together—were wasted. Because he wouldn't consider marriage. You see, your mother had crushed him in that aspect. He was afraid to try to be a husband again. Afraid to reach for the happiness he so deserved. I don't want that to happen to you, Mariah. I don't want the best years of your life to be wasted because of fear or pride or doubts."

Amazed at Linda's revelation, Mariah reached over and placed her hand on the woman's forearm. "I feel like a fool. It never dawned on me that you loved Dad in that way. I never realized that Dad loved you. I always thought you two were just very good friends. Now, I only wish—oh, Linda, you would've made him the perfect wife. And Aimee and I needed you—as a mother." She shook her head with regret. "You're right. Dad wasted so many years."

Leaning forward, Linda gently touched her hand to Mariah's cheeks. "You love Finn. Go to him. Tell him that, if nothing else. Then if it's meant for you to be together, it will happen."

Could Linda be right? Could there be a chance that Finn really loved her?

"Me go to him?" she asked dazedly.

Linda gave her a wry smile. "You're the one who sent him away."

Go to Nevada and face Finn? What would she tell him? How could she make him understand that all she'd ever wanted was his love? She didn't know. She only knew she had to try.

Rising to her feet, she wrapped her arms around the other woman. "I love you," she said thickly.

Linda patted her back. "Ray would be proud of you. And so am I."

Chapter Twelve

Two days later, Finn stood next to his sister as they gazed across an open section of the J Bar J. A few yards away, his herd of mustangs was grazing on the summer grasses that were currently flourishing after a flurry of unexpected rain showers had hit the area.

"The babies are sturdy little things," Sassy said as one paint colt kicked up his heels and began to run circles around his mother. "Look at that. He thinks he belongs on the racetrack."

Finn grunted with amusement. The sight of the babies was bittersweet. They were all safely born now. And all growing like weeds. He was proud of his expanding herd. And at one time, he'd believed Mariah had been proud, too. But he'd been wrong about her feelings for the horses. And her feelings for him.

"That guy won't be going to a track. But he might

turn into a nice roping horse." He glanced at Sassy. "Just bear with me, sis. I promise you'll have your pasture back soon. Tomorrow I'm going to look at some land east of here. Actually, it's not far from Grandma and Grandpa Reeves. It might not be exactly what I need, but I'll know when I see it."

Sassy wrapped her hands around his upper arm and gave it a hard yank. "I've told you over and over, Finn. There's no hurry. In fact, I'm loving having them here. You wouldn't want to sell them to me, would you?"

He rolled his eyes at her. "Not hardly. Maybe when I get a big herd I'll give you a few. How's that?"

She pressed her cheek against his arm. "I might just take you up on that, brother. But in the meantime, what is Dad saying about this step you're taking to get a place of your own?"

"He's coming around. Gramps isn't happy about it. But he won't say much. What can he say? I'm thirty-two years old."

Sassy stepped back and gave him a long, searching look. "Well, I'm glad you're going on with your plans. But to be honest, you look awful, Finn. In fact, I've never seen you looking so drawn and—well, sad. I'm worried about you. And so is Jett."

Finn grimaced. Since he'd come home from California he'd tried his best to return to normal, to be the same happy-go-lucky guy he'd been before he'd met Mariah and his son. But nothing felt the same. He was a different man now. And though he wanted to believe he'd changed for the better, he actually felt like a gullible fool. He'd let one Montgomery sister seduce him, then he'd turned right around and let the second sister snag a hold of his heart.

"Guess my acting ability needs work. I thought I was putting on a pretty good show of being happy. Not convincing enough, huh?"

Sassy shook her head. "Not even a little."

Taking her by the arm, he urged her in the direction of the truck. "We'd better get back to the house. Gypsy is going to be pulling her hair out trying to see after three kids."

Sassy walked a few steps with him, then stopped. "Gypsy could handle five kids if need be. And we're going to stand right here in the middle of the pasture until you tell me what's going on. Is it Harry's aunt? Are you feeling guilty or something about taking Harry from her?"

With a painful groan, Finn looked toward the sky. There wasn't a cloud to be seen and the sun was hot on his face. Normally this was the kind of day that made him want to jump a fence or sing at the top of his lungs. Instead, he felt as though the heavy weight in his heart would never lift.

"Or something," he muttered. "I don't want to talk about her. Or California. Or anything about it. I have Harry now. It's over and done with."

His pretty redheaded sister folded her arms against her chest in a stance of defiance. "Too bad if you don't want to talk. There was a time a few years ago when I didn't want to talk, either. I was pregnant and afraid—especially afraid that no one in the Calhoun family really wanted me around. And Jett—I couldn't believe that a man like him might really love me. You forced me to talk about those things, and if you hadn't—well, I shudder to think that I might have turned my back on this wonderful life I have now."

His expression softened as he studied her face. Several years ago, no one in the Calhoun family had known Sassy existed. But she'd come here from New Mexico on a hunch. Someone had told her that she looked like Finn and she'd wondered if there was some sort of connection between her and the Calhoun family. The moment he'd first laid eyes on her, Finn had been certain she was his sister, and he'd fought to get the truth revealed.

In doing so, he and Sassy had opened up a dark family secret. Not only had the Calhoun brothers learned that Orin had been unfaithful to their mother, they'd also learned their grandfather Bart had schemed to keep the affair and Sassy's birth a secret. But time had a way of sweeping things into the past. Orin and Bart had been forgiven and Sassy had become a cherished member of the family.

"That's true," Finn admitted. "I did force you to open up and face things that I'm not sure I would've been brave enough to face. I even talked you into the DNA test. And if I bullied you a bit, I'm not sorry. I have my sister now."

"And your sister wants you to be happy. So talk. What is the problem with Mariah?"

Frowning, he turned and stared hollowly at the herd of horses. "She isn't the problem. I guess I am. I made a fool of myself. I proposed to her—believing that she loved me. She turned me down. And—well, after that she wanted me to leave Stallion Canyon as soon as I could. So I did. I got Harry and my horses and came home."

"But now this doesn't feel like home to you anymore. Right?"

Finn turned back to his sister. "How did you know that?"

She smiled slyly. "Because once I met Jett, New Mexico didn't feel like home anymore to me."

"You're too smart, sis," he said glumly.

Stepping forward, she grabbed up his hand and squeezed it between both of hers. "I'm just a good guesser," she told him. "And I'm guessing that Mariah does love you. Otherwise, she wouldn't have made an issue of you leaving. Did she give you a reason for turning you down?"

Finn grimaced. "She believes I was after her ranch," he muttered, then shook his head with frustration. "And maybe I did botch the way I proposed to her. Maybe it was insensitive of me to mention the ranch at all. But it's where I wanted us to make our home. Was that so wrong?"

Sassy gave his hand a hard tug. "Finn, a woman wants to know that she's loved just for herself. You need to convince Mariah that you'd be happy to live with her anywhere. You would be, wouldn't you?"

He nodded soberly. "Nowhere on this earth would make me happy unless she was with me."

With a big smile, Sassy urged him into a walk. "Then you need to tell her that. And I don't mean pick up the phone and call her. You need to take her into your arms and show her."

He cast her a doubtful glance. "Do you think she'll listen?"

Sassy chuckled softly. "I'd be willing to bet twelve of my new calves against your mustangs that she'll listen."

Finn suddenly urged her into a faster walk back to the truck. "Come on, slowpoke. I've got to get to the Horn and start making arrangements to drive back to Alturas."

Laughing, Sassy turned loose of his hand and started

trotting the last few yards to the waiting pickup truck. "Thank God I have my brother back!"

Back on the Silver Horn, after Finn turned Harry over to Tessa, he hurried down to the horse barn to discuss his schedule with Colley, the Horn's head horse trainer and Finn's right-hand man.

As the two men stood outside the open doorway of Finn's office, Finn informed the rugged cowboy of his plans. "I'm not certain how long I'll be gone. Maybe just a day. Or it might be several. Either way I'll make sure Rafe and Dad keep in close touch with you."

"Don't worry about anything, Finn. We'll be working on the yearlings for the next few days. And Rafe wants us to rotate the remuda to another pasture. So we'll be doing that, too."

"Sounds good," Finn told him. "I'll see you when—"

Finn broke off as a flash of movement at the opposite end of the barn caught the corner of his eye. Glancing down the wide alleyway, he peered through the dim, dusty light. Beyond a stable hand pushing a wheelbarrow full of dirty shavings, a woman was walking in their direction. And she looked incredibly like Mariah.

"What's the matter?" Colley turned his head to follow Finn's stare. "Oh. Is she here to buy horses?"

For a moment, Finn wasn't sure he was going to be able to answer Colley's question. His throat had gone so tight he could scarcely breathe.

"Uh, no. That's Harry's aunt." He jerked his gaze back to the cowboy. "Would you excuse me, Colley? I'll talk to you later."

The man gave Mariah one last curious glance. "Sure, Finn. I'll be out with the yearlings."

Colley walked away while Finn stood where he was, watching in disbelief as Mariah came to a stop a few feet in front of him. She was wearing a white cotton sundress with pink and yellow flowers splashed over the full skirt. A pink silk scarf had been twisted into a tight cord and wrapped around her black hair to keep it off her face. She was the loveliest thing he'd ever seen in his life, and he suddenly prayed for the right words to come to him.

"Hello, Finn. I just came from the house. Tessa told me I could probably find you here at the barn. Am I interrupting anything?"

Only his whole life, he thought.

"No. That was my assistant. I'll finish my conversation with him later." He stepped toward her and his heart was suddenly pounding so hard he could hear a whooshing noise in his ears. "You must be here to see Harry. He's going to be happy to see you."

She moved closer and Finn folded his hands into fists to keep from reaching out and grabbing her. She looked so incredibly soft and womanly. And the sweet scent drifting from her called up all sorts of evocative memories.

"I do want to see Harry. But that's not why I came here today," she said.

Doubts and uncertainties were practically paralyzing him. His brain felt frozen, and even if the barn suddenly caught fire, he doubted he could move a muscle.

"Why are you here?" he finally managed to ask.

"You."

She'd spoken the word so lowly that he barely heard it. But it was enough to send a thrill of hope rushing through him. Or was he getting way ahead of himself?

Maybe she was here to tell him she wanted partial custody of Harry? But that didn't make sense. Not when she'd always insisted Harry needed to be with his father.

He gestured toward the open doorway behind him, all the while aware that two young grooms leading a pair of yearlings down the alleyway had stopped to stare at Mariah. It wasn't unusual for women to visit the horse barn. The Silver Horn probably sold more horses to women than men. But Mariah was different from those women. Seeing her in this dusty barn was like spotting a violet in the middle of a prickly pear patch.

"My office is right here," he told her. "We can talk in private."

She moved past him and stepped into the room. Finn followed right behind her and was amazed to find that his legs were trembling as though he'd just run several miles at a torrid pace.

"How did you get here? Drive?" he asked.

"Yes. I left early this morning," she said as he carefully shut the door behind him. "I'm sorry about showing up without warning. I started to call. But I was afraid you might tell me not to come."

He walked over to his desk and rested a hip on one corner. She continued to stand awkwardly in the middle of the room and Finn could only wonder how she would react if he closed the short distance between them and pulled her into his arms. Would she remind him that their lovemaking had ended back at Stallion Canyon?

"Why would you think I'd do that?" he asked.

She made a helpless gesture with her hands. "We— uh—didn't exactly part on pleasant terms."

He swallowed as his mind was suddenly consumed with the pain he'd endured these past weeks. Losing her had turned his skies gray. He wanted to see the sun again. He wanted to believe that the magic they'd shared on Stallion Canyon had never died.

"No. There was nothing pleasant about leaving you or Stallion Canyon," he confessed. "So what are you going to say now? That I'm still after your ranch?"

"If I truly believed that I wouldn't be here."

His gaze locked with hers and before he knew it, he was crossing the small space between them and wrapping his hands around her shoulders.

"I don't know why you're here, Mariah," he said hoarsely. "But I have to tell you—"

"Wait, Finn!" She touched her fingertips to his cheek. "Before you say anything, I have to tell you—I'm here because I love you. I should've told you that from the very beginning. But I was mixed up and so afraid."

"Afraid? Oh, Mariah, there wasn't any reason for you to be afraid. Not of me."

Her head moved back and forth as tears began to fill her eyes. "It wasn't you, Finn. I was doubting myself. When you told me you loved me—that you wanted for us to get married—I couldn't believe it. You see, I've always thought of myself as the forgotten daughter—the second-best sister. Compared to Aimee I was the quiet wallflower who rarely got noticed."

He gave her shoulders a gentle shake. "That's ridiculous, Mariah. You're a beautiful, intelligent woman with so much to offer. I'm sure there have been plenty of guys who'd give their eyeteeth to date you."

Her gaze slipped to the middle of his chest and Finn could suddenly see the raw vulnerability on her features. The sight made his heart ache, made him want to wrap her in a tight hold and shield her from every hurtful thing in the world.

"A few," she said quietly. "But once they met Aimee I was usually forgotten."

"That's hard for me to believe."

"I imagined it would be. That's why I never said anything. But now I have to tell you how things were back then. So that maybe you'll understand."

"Tell me what?" he urged.

She sighed. "The reason why my engagement ended all those years ago. You see, when I met Kris during my college studies, I thought he was different. When he proposed and gave me a beautiful engagement ring, I thought finally someone loved me just for being me."

"But something happened."

Nodding, she said, "We were about to set the date for the wedding when Aimee started insisting she couldn't let me make a mistake. She kept telling me Kris was no good. Which didn't make sense. When we'd first gotten engaged, she'd thought he was a great catch for me. I finally demanded that she explain herself and that's when she admitted that she'd been sleeping with Kris. That she'd seduced him as a test to determine whether he was going to be faithful to me and he'd failed."

Finn felt sick. "Oh God, Mariah, I can't imagine what that must've done to you. But I'm guessing that you forgave your sister. You have that kind of heart. It's why I fell in love with you."

She let out a long breath and lifted her gaze back to him. Tears were still in her eyes and as she tried to blink them away, they dropped like wet diamonds onto her cheeks. "Yes, I forgave her. But I couldn't forget. After that, I couldn't trust her. And I especially couldn't trust another man. So when you started talking about love and marriage—it all came crashing at me."

He nodded glumly. "And I'd already had a brief affair with Aimee. And had a baby with her. You must've been feeling like you were my second choice."

Hope suddenly lit her gray eyes. "Then—you do understand?"

Groaning, he pulled her into his arms and pressed his cheek against the top of her head. "I do now," he murmured.

"Oh, Finn, I've been so miserable without you. I've been moping about, wondering how I could go on without you and Harry."

"What made you finally decide to drive down here?"

"You can give Linda the credit for opening my eyes. She convinced me I'd be making a huge mistake if I let you get away from me."

The joy surging through Finn couldn't be contained, and for the first time since they'd parted, he was able to put a genuine smile on his face. "I wasn't going to get away from you, my darling. When you walked up a few minutes ago, I was explaining to Colley that I was leaving for California in the morning."

Her head reared back as she stared wondrously up at him. "For California! To see me?"

He laughed at her dismay. "Yes. To see you. Sassy did some convincing with me, too. She told me I'd be a fool if I didn't do something to win you back." Pressing his lips to her forehead, he said, "I'm so sorry, Mariah. I made such a mess of things that night when I proposed. Nothing about it was right. I shouldn't have mentioned the ranch. I shouldn't have said anything—except that I love you and want you to be my wife. It doesn't matter where we live. As long as we're together."

With a rueful shake of her head, she reached up and tenderly cradled his face with both hands. "No, Finn. You didn't make a mess of things," she said huskily. "Everything you said was right—and beautiful. I was just too blinded with self-doubt to let myself see the love on your face. Can you forgive me?"

"I already have. Now, tell me, are you going to marry me?"

Smiling, she slipped her arms around his waist and pressed herself tight against him. "Yes. As soon as you'd like."

"How about tomorrow?" he asked excitedly. "We can drive down to Vegas, get married, and catch a plane to anywhere you'd like for our honeymoon."

"Tomorrow? I don't have a dress with me. Except the one I have on."

"As far as I'm concerned you look perfect in it. But I'll buy you a dress for the wedding. I'll buy you a dozen dresses and whatever else you'll need while we're away."

"Hmm. That's quite an offer," she said slyly, her eyes gleaming. "And I can choose where we go on our honeymoon?"

"That's right. Hawaii, Europe, Australia, anywhere. Just name it."

"All right, since you're letting me choose, what would you say about us going back to Stallion Canyon?"

Uncertain, he stared at her. "Are you serious?"

She nodded. "I'm very serious. Now that the three of us are going to be living there as a family, Stallion Canyon is going to be a new and exciting place for us.

Can you think of a better place for us to go for a honeymoon?"

For a moment Finn was so overwhelmed with emotion he couldn't speak. All he could do was press her head against his chest, stroke her hair and savor the amazing joy filling his heart.

"I don't deserve you, my darling," he finally managed to whisper. "But I promise that you will always come first in my life. You and our children. The horses, the land, the ranch, they'll be a distant second. You do believe that, don't you?"

"I do," she said, then tilting her head back, she smiled impishly up at him. "But I won't mind you proving it from time to time."

"Mmm. What a pleasure that will be."

Bending his head, he kissed her. A kiss that bound their future together. A future that spread before them like a bright, beautiful sunrise.

"Finn, what—"

Finn's head jerked up, and over Mariah's head, he saw his father standing in the doorway. From Orin's expression, he was clearly shocked to find his son with a woman in his arms.

"Sorry for the interruption," Orin said awkwardly. "I'll come back later."

"Don't go," Finn said quickly. "You've actually shown up at a great time."

His expression full of questions, Orin entered the room and Mariah stepped out of Finn's arms to face her future father-in-law.

"Dad, this is Mariah," Finn explained. "She's just agreed to marry me."

Mariah quickly walked over and extended her hand to Orin. "It's nice to finally meet you, Mr. Calhoun."

Pressing her hand between his, he gave Finn a crooked grin. "I can see what you've been pining for now." He turned his attention back to Mariah. "Welcome to the family, Mariah. I've no doubts that you and Finn will be very happy."

"Very happy," Mariah agreed, then glanced coyly at Finn. "Raising mustangs."

Moving up behind her, Finn wrapped his arm around Mariah's shoulder and drew her close to his side. "And babies," Finn added. "Let's not forget those."

"I doubt you'll let me forget that part of our bargain," she teased.

Orin shot Finn a perceptive look. "Besides giving me more grandchildren, I have a feeling my new daughter-in-law is going to change my mind about those damned wild horses."

Laughing softly, she said, "I'll be disappointed if you don't come visit us often, Mr. Calhoun."

"I'm not Mr. Calhoun," he told her. "Call me Dad. We're going to be family."

She smiled at Orin, then looked up at Finn. Her eyes were glittering with happy tears.

"Yes," she murmured. "One big family. For always."

Epilogue

Six months later, on a cold November night, Finn and Mariah were in the kitchen of Stallion Canyon's ranch house, preparing for tomorrow and the big Thanksgiving meal they planned to share with some of Finn's family. The smell of baking pumpkin pies filled the room, and holiday music played softly on the radio. While Mariah stood at the cabinet counter peeling boiled eggs to put into the dressing, Finn washed a sink full of pots and pans. Across the room, Harry, who'd been walking for the past two weeks, was squealing with delight as he tried to keep up with a collie pup.

Mariah placed the last egg into an airtight container before she glanced over her shoulder at Harry. The toddler had managed to catch the collie, or the pup had simply tired of the game of tag. Presently, boy and dog were now cuddled together on a braided rug near the breakfast bar.

"You made our son one happy little boy when you brought that puppy home to him," she told Finn. "Look, he's stroking Samson's head exactly how you showed him."

"Naturally," Finn said proudly. "He's a smart little boy. And our next son will probably be brilliant, too."

Smiling, Mariah's hand slipped to the growing mound of her waistline. A month after she and Finn were married, she'd gotten pregnant. Now that she was five months along, Finn was already making plans to turn one of the larger bedrooms in the house into a nursery big enough to hold Harry and the new baby.

"You don't know if this one is a boy," she reminded her husband. "Remember, we didn't want the doctor to tell us. It's going to be a surprise."

"I confess. I called him a few days ago without you knowing and asked him to spill the beans," Finn teased. "The baby is going to be a boy."

Mariah chuckled as she placed a stalk of celery on a chopping board. "You're telling a whopper. And what are you going to say when the baby turns out to be a girl?"

He gave her a broad grin. "Yippee! That's what I'll say. And right now I say you've been on your feet for too long. You need to sit."

"I have a few more things to do here first," she protested. "And I feel fine."

He stepped over and took her by the arm. "Don't argue. You can finish things here in the kitchen after you rest a few minutes."

With Harry and the puppy leading the way, they made their way to the living room, where Finn guided Mariah over to a big stuffed armchair. Once she'd sunk into the soft leather, he propped her feet on a matching footstool.

"There. Comfy now?" he asked.

She patted the wide armrest of the chair. "I'll be even more comfy if you sit down here beside me."

"Okay. For a minute. And then I'm going to go make you a cup of hot chocolate. You need the extra milk."

She let out a good-natured groan. "Finn, you fuss over me more than you do your pregnant mares."

Leaning over her, he slid his forefinger beneath her chin. "You're number one to me. Didn't I promise that you'd always be number one?"

Tilting her head back, she smiled dreamily up at him. "Yes. And you've kept your promise."

She reached for his hand and drew it to her lips. The past six months of being Finn's wife had changed her life in the most wonderful way. Harry was happy and healthy. Their new baby was coming soon and Finn was slowly and surely building Stallion Canyon into the ranch he'd always wanted. He'd made several profitable sales in the past couple of months, but he'd used most of that to purchase more of the wild horses in order to keep building the herd.

Seeing the ranch return to a thriving business had lifted Mariah's spirits more than she could've ever guessed, and she thanked God every day that a buyer hadn't come along before she and Finn had married. As for her teaching job, she was still enjoying being in the classroom on a daily basis. And with Linda more than glad to help her with Harry and the coming baby, she didn't see any reason to give up a job that was an important part of her life.

She let out a contented sigh. "We haven't had a big Thanksgiving dinner in this house for several years. It's wonderful to be celebrating again. And I'm so excited about Dad and Rafe and his family coming tomorrow to spend a few days with us. I only wish Sassy and Jett could come with them."

"With Sassy's baby due any day now it wouldn't be safe for her to travel. But she promises to come soon and bring the whole brood with her. I'll have to erect bunk beds in the big bedroom to sleep them all," he joked. "Or maybe I should forget the bunk beds and send them all out to the barn to sleep on the hay."

They both laughed before Finn looked over to make sure Harry and Samson weren't getting into trouble.

"Look at those two," Finn said softly. "I think they're going to be the best of buddies."

Mariah glanced over to see Harry and the puppy curled up together, asleep on the rug in front of the fireplace. The precious sight put a smile in her heart. "I'll get a blanket and cover them," she said. "It's warm there in front of the fire, but just in case there's a draft on the floor."

Before she could rise, Finn put a hand on her arm and rose to his feet. "I'll do it. I'm going after the hot chocolate anyway."

Minutes later he returned from the kitchen to find Mariah staring out the window at the frosty night.

"What are you thinking?" he asked softly as he knelt next to her chair and handed her the mug of hot chocolate.

A wistful smile touched the corners of her lips. "Actually, I was thinking of Aimee."

"Oh. I hope you're not about to get sad on me. Thanksgiving is supposed to be a joyful time. A time to appreciate all our blessings."

"I'm not getting sad. I was remembering some of the nice times we had together as sisters growing up.

Dad gave us a puppy once, too. She looked almost like Samson. We adored her." She sipped the hot drink, then glanced gratefully at Finn. "Aimee was a troubled young woman. But I loved her in spite of everything."

He gave her shoulder a loving squeeze. "I made a big mistake by getting involved with her. But on the other hand I can't regret it. If not for Aimee, I wouldn't have Harry. I would've never met you, my darling wife. And our new baby wouldn't be on the way. Strange as it seems, we owe her for bringing us together."

"That's true," Mariah said. "And tomorrow I think we should light a special candle for Aimee. She might just be able to see it. After all, it is a time for giving thanks."

Finn leaned over and softly kissed her lips. "And I'm thankful every day that I have you and our son, my love."

* * * * *

THIS WAS HER favorite kind of Haven Point evening.

McKenzie Shaw locked the front door of her shop, Point Made Flowers and Gifts. The day had been long and hectic, filled with customers and orders, which was wonderful, but also plenty of unavoidable mayoral business.

She was tired and wanted to stretch out on the terrace or her beloved swing, with her feet up and something cool at her elbow. The image beckoned but the sweetness of the view in front of her made her pause.

"Hold on," she said to Paprika, her cinnamon standard poodle. The dog gave her a long-suffering look but settled next to the bench in front of the store.

McKenzie sat and reached a hand down to pet Rika's curly hair. A few sailboats cut through the stunning blue waters of Lake Haven, silvery and bright in the fading light, with the rugged, snowcapped mountains as a backdrop.

She didn't stop nearly often enough to soak in the beautiful view or enjoy the June evening air, tart and clean from the mighty fir and pines growing in abundance around the lake.

A tourist couple walked past holding hands and eating gelato cones from Carmela's, their hair backlit into golden halos by the setting sun. From a short distance away, she could hear children laughing and shrieking as they played on the beach at the city park and the alluring scent of grilling steak somewhere close by made her stomach grumble.

She loved every season here on the lake but the magnificent Haven Point summers were her favorite—especially lazy summer evenings filled with long shadows and spectacular sunsets.

Kayaking on the lake, watching children swim out to the floating docks, seeing old-timers in ancient boats casting gossamer lines out across the water. It was all part of the magic of Haven Point's short summer season.

The town heavily depended on the influx of tourists during the summer, though it didn't come close to the crowds enjoyed by their larger city to the north, Shelter Springs—especially since the Haven Point Inn burned down just before Christmas and had yet to be rebuilt.

Shelter Springs had more available lodging, more restaurants, more shopping—as well as more problems with parking, traffic congestion and crime, she reminded herself.

"Evening, Mayor," Mike Bailey called, waving as

he rumbled past the store in the gorgeous old blue '57 Chevy pickup he'd restored.

She waved back, then nodded to Luis Ayala, locking up his insurance agency across the street.

A soft, warm feeling of contentment seeped through her. This was her town, these were her people. She was part of it, just like the Redemption Mountains across the lake. She had fought to earn that sense of belonging since the day she showed up, a lost, grieving, bewildered girl.

She had worked hard to earn the respect of her friends and neighbors. The chance to serve as the mayor had never been something she sought but she had accepted the challenge willingly. It wasn't about power or influence—not that one could find much of either in a small town like Haven Point. She simply wanted to do anything she could to make a difference in her community. She wanted to think she was serving with honor and dignity, but she was fully aware there were plenty in town who might disagree.

Her stomach growled, louder this time. That steak smelled as if it was charred to perfection. Too bad she didn't know who was grilling it or she might just stop by to say hello. McKenzie was briefly tempted to stop in at Serrano's or even grab a gelato of her own at Carmela's—stracciatella, her particular favorite—but she decided she would be better off taking Rika home.

"Come on, girl. Let's go."

The dog jumped to her feet, all eager, lanky grace, and McKenzie gripped the leash and headed off.

She lived not quite a mile from her shop downtown and she and Rika both looked forward all day to this evening walk along the trail that circled the lake.

As she walked, she waved at people walking, biking, driving, even boating past when the shoreline came into view. It was quite a workout for her arm but she didn't mind. Each wave was another reminder that this was her town and she loved it.

"Let's grill some chicken when we get home," she said aloud to Rika, whose tongue lolled out with appropriate enthusiasm.

Talking to her dog again. Not a good sign but she decided it was too beautiful an evening to worry about her decided lack of any social life to speak of. Town council meetings absolutely didn't count.

WHEN SHE REACHED her lakeside house, however, she discovered a luxury SUV with California plates in the driveway of the house next to hers, with boat trailer and gleaming wooden boat attached.

Great.

Apparently someone had rented the Sloane house.

Normally she would be excited about new neighbors but in this case, she knew the tenants would only be temporary. Since moving to Shelter Springs, Carole Sloane-Hall had been renting out the house she received as a settlement in her divorce for a furnished vacation rental. Sometimes people stayed for a week or two, sometimes only a few days.

It was a lovely home, probably one of the most luxurious lakefront rentals within the city limits. Though not large, it had huge windows overlooking the lake, a wide flagstone terrace and a semiprivate boat dock—which, unfortunately, was shared between McKenzie's own property and Carole's rental house.

She wouldn't let it spoil her evening, she told herself. Usually the renters were very nice people, quiet and polite. She generally tried to act as friendly and welcoming as possible.

It wouldn't bother her at all except the two properties had virtually an open backyard because both needed access to the shared dock, with only some landscaping between the houses that ended several yards from the high watermark. Sometimes she found the lack of privacy a little disconcerting, with strangers temporarily living next door, but Carole assured her she planned to put the house on the market at the end of the summer. With everything else McKenzie had to worry about, she had relegated the vacation rental situation next door to a distant corner of her brain.

New neighbors or not, though, she still adored her own house. She had purchased it two years earlier and still felt a little rush of excitement when she unlocked the front door and walked over the threshold.

Over those two years, she had worked hard to make it her own, sprucing it up with new paint, taking down a few walls and adding one in a better spot. The biggest expense had been for the renovated master bath, which now contained a huge claw-foot tub, and the new kitchen with warm travertine countertops and the intricately tiled backsplash she had done herself.

This was hers and she loved every inch of it, almost more than she loved her little store downtown.

She walked through to the back door and let Rika off her leash. Though the yard was only fenced on one side, just as the Sloane house was fenced on the corresponding outer property edge, Rika was well trained and never left the yard.

Her cell phone rang as she was throwing together a quick lemon-tarragon marinade for the chicken.

Some days, she wanted to grab her kayak, paddle out to the middle of Lake Haven—where it was rumored to be so deep, the bottom had never been truly charted— and toss the stupid thing overboard.

This time when she saw the caller ID, she smiled, wiped her hands on a dish towel and quickly answered. "Hey, Devin."

"Hey, sis. I can't believe you're holding out on me! Come on. Doesn't your favorite sister get to be among the first to hear?"

She tucked the phone in her shoulder and returned to cutting the lemon for the marinade as she mentally reviewed her day for anything spill-worthy to her sister.

The store had been busy enough. She had busted the doddering and not-quite-right Mrs. Anglesey for trying to walk out of the store without paying for the pretty hand-beaded bracelet she tried on when she came into the store with her daughter.

But that sort of thing was a fairly regular occurrence whenever Beth and her mother came into the store and was handled easily enough, with flustered apologies from Beth and that baffled "what did I do wrong?" look from poor Mrs. Anglesey.

She didn't think Devin would be particularly interested in that or the great commission she'd earned by selling one of the beautiful carved horses an artist friend made in the woodshop behind his house to a tourist from Maine.

And then there was the pleasant encounter with Mr. Twitchell, but she doubted that was what her sister meant.

"Sorry. You lost me somewhere. I can't think of any news I have worth sharing."

"Seriously? You didn't think I would want to know that Ben Kilpatrick is back in town?"

The knife slipped from her hands and she narrowly avoided chopping the tip of her finger off. A greasy, angry ball formed in her stomach.

Ben Kilpatrick. The only person on earth she could honestly say she despised. She picked up the knife and stabbed it through the lemon, wishing it was his cold, black heart.

"You're joking," she said, though she couldn't imagine what her sister would find remotely funny about making up something so outlandish and horrible.

"True story," Devin assured her. "I heard it from Betty Orton while I was getting gas. Apparently he strolled into the grocery store a few hours ago, casual as a Sunday morning, and bought what looked to be at least a week's worth of groceries. She said he didn't look very happy to be back. He just frowned when she welcomed him back."

"It's a mistake. That's all. She mistook him for someone else."

"That's what I said, but Betty assured me she's known him all his life and taught him in Sunday school three years in a row and she's not likely to mistake him for someone else."

"I won't believe it until I see him," she said. "He hates

Haven Point. That's fairly obvious, since he's done his best to drive our town into the ground."

"Not actively," Devin, who tended to see the good in just about everyone, was quick to point out.

"What's the difference? By completely ignoring the property he inherited after his father died, he accomplished the same thing as if he'd walked up and down Lake Street, setting a torch to the whole downtown."

She picked up the knife and started chopping the fresh tarragon with quick, angry movements. "You know how hard it's been the last five years since he inherited to keep tenants in the downtown businesses. Haven Point is dying because of one person. Ben Kilpatrick."

If she had only one goal for her next four years as mayor, she dreamed of revitalizing a town whose lifeblood was seeping away, business by business.

When she was a girl, downtown Haven Point had been bustling with activity, a magnet for everyone in town, with several gift and clothing boutiques for both men and women, restaurants and cafés, even a downtown movie theater.

She still ached when she thought of it, when she looked around at all the empty storefronts and the ramshackle buildings with peeling paint and broken shutters.

"It's his fault we've lost so many businesses and nothing has moved in to replace them. I mean, why go to all the trouble to open a business," she demanded, "if the landlord is going to be completely unresponsive and won't fix even the most basic problems?"

"You don't have to sell it to me, Kenz. I know. I went to your campaign rallies, remember?"

"Right. Sorry." It was definitely one of her hot

buttons. She loved Haven Point and hated seeing its decline—much like old Mrs. Anglesey, who had once been an elegant, respected, contributing member of the community and now could barely get around even with her daughter's help and didn't remember whether she had paid for items in the store.

"It wasn't really his fault, anyway. He hired an incompetent crook of a property manager who was supposed to be taking care of things. It wasn't Ben's fault the man embezzled from him and didn't do the necessary upkeep to maintain the buildings."

"Oh, come on. Ben Kilpatrick is the chief operating officer for one of the most successful, fastest-growing companies in the world. You think he didn't know what was going on? If he had bothered to care, he would have paid more attention."

This was an argument she and Devin had had before. "At some point, you're going to have to let go," her sister said calmly. "Ben doesn't own any part of Haven Point now. He sold everything to Aidan Caine last year— which makes his presence in town even more puzzling. Why would he come back *now*, after all these years? It would seem to me, he has even *less* reason to show his face in town now."

McKenzie still wasn't buying the rumor that Ben had actually returned. He had been gone since he was seventeen years old. He didn't even come back for Joe Kilpatrick's funeral five years earlier—though she, for one, wasn't super surprised about that since Joe had been a bastard to everyone in town and especially to his only surviving child.

"It doesn't make any sense. What possible reason would he have to come back now?"

"I don't know. Maybe he's here to make amends. Did you ever think of that?"

How could he ever make amends for what he had done to Haven Point—not to mention shattering all her girlish illusions?

Of course, she didn't mention that to Devin as she tossed the tarragon into the lemon juice while her sister continued speculating about Ben's motives for coming back to town.

Her sister probably had no idea about McKenzie's ridiculous crush on Ben, that when she was younger, she had foolishly considered him her ideal guy. Just thinking about it now made her cringe.

Yes, he had been gorgeous enough. Vivid blue eyes, long sooty eyelashes, the old clichéd chiseled jaw—not to mention that lock of sun-streaked brown hair that always seemed to be falling into his eyes, just begging for the right girl to push it back, like Belle did to the Prince after the Beast in her arms suddenly materialized into him.

Throw in that edge of pain she always sensed in him and his unending kindness and concern for his sickly younger sister and it was no wonder her thirteen-year-old self—best friends with that same sister—used to pine for him to notice her, despite the four-year difference in their ages.

It was so stupid, she didn't like admitting it, even to herself. All that had been an illusion, obviously. He might have been sweet and solicitous to Lily but that was his only redeeming quality. His actions these past five years had proved that, over and over.

Through the open kitchen window, she heard Rika start barking fiercely, probably at some poor hapless chipmunk or squirrel that dared venture into her territory.

"I'd better go," she said to Devin. "Rika's mad at something."

"Yeah, I've got to go, too. Looks like the Shelter Springs ambulance is on its way with a cardiac patient."

"Okay. Good luck. Go save a life."

Her sister was a dedicated, caring doctor at Lake Haven Hospital, as passionate about her patients as McKenzie was about their town.

"Let me know if you hear anything down at city hall about why Ben Kilpatrick has come back to our fair city after all these years."

"Sure. And then maybe you can tell me why you're so curious."

She could almost hear the shrug in Devin's voice. "Are you kidding me? It's not every day a gorgeous playboy billionaire comes to town."

And that was the crux of the matter. Somehow it seemed wholly unfair, a serious Karmic calamity, that he had done so well for himself after he left town. If she had her way, he would be living in the proverbial van down by the river—or at least in one of his own dilapidated buildings.

Rika barked again and McKenzie hurried to the back door that led onto her terrace. She really hoped it wasn't a skunk. They weren't uncommon in the area, especially not this time of year. Her dog had encountered one the week before on their morning run on a favorite mountain trail and it had taken her three baths in the magic solution she found on the internet before she could allow Rika back into the house.

Her dog wasn't in the yard, she saw immediately. Now that she was outside, she realized the barking was more excited and playful than upset. All the more reason to hope she wasn't trying to make nice with some odiferous little friend.

"Come," she called again. "Inside."

The dog bounded through a break in the bushes between the house next door, followed instantly by another dog—a beautiful German shepherd with classic markings.

She had been right. Rika *had* been making friends. She and the German shepherd looked tight as ticks, tails wagging as they raced exuberantly around the yard.

The dog must belong to the new renters of the Sloane house. Carol would pitch a royal fit if she knew they had a dog over there. McKenzie knew it was strictly prohibited.

Now what was she supposed to do?

A man suddenly walked through the gap in landscaping. He had brown hair, but a sudden piercing ray of the setting sun obscured his features more than that.

She *really* didn't want a confrontation with the man, especially not on a Friday night when she had been so looking forward to a relaxing night at home. She supposed she could just call Carole or the property management company and let them deal with the situation.

That seemed a cop-out since Carole had asked her to keep an eye on the place.

She forced a smile and approached the dog's owner. "Hi. Good evening. You must be renting the place from Carole. I'm McKenzie Shaw. I live next door. Rika, that dog you're playing catch with, is mine."

The man turned around and the pleasant evening around her seemed to go dark and still as she took in brown sun-streaked hair, steely blue eyes, chiseled jaw.

Her stomach dropped as if somebody had just picked her up and tossed her into the cold lake.

Ben Kilpatrick. Here. Staying in the house next door. So much for her lovely evening at home.

* * * * *

Don't miss
REDEMPTION BAY by RaeAnne Thayne,
available July 2015 wherever
HQN Books are sold.
www.HQNBooks.com

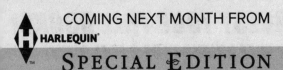

REQUEST YOUR FREE BOOKS!
2 FREE NOVELS PLUS 2 FREE GIFTS!

H HARLEQUIN®

SPECIAL EDITION

Life, Love & Family

"You don't mind if I see her?" he asked uncertainly.

"No, I don't mind," Claire answered in the same quiet
voice. She gestured toward the baby lying in the portable
playpen. "Go on, it's okay. Since Bekka lights up whenever you walk into a room, maybe it might be a good
thing for her if you spent a little time with our little girl."

"Thanks," Levi said to her with feeling. Then he slanted
another look toward Claire—a longer one as he tried to
puzzle things out—and asked, "How do you feel about
my spending time with her mother?"

Claire arched one eyebrow as she regarded him. "I
wouldn't push it if I were you, Levi," she warned.

He raised his hands in a sign of complete surrender.
"Message received. You don't need to say another word,
Claire. My question is officially rescinded," he told her.

And then, because he prided himself on always being truthful with Claire, he added, "I'm a patient man. I can wait until you decide to change your mind about that."

Because he had really left her no recourse if she was to save face, Claire told him, "I don't think there's enough patience in the whole world for that."

"We'll see," Levi said softly, more to himself than to her. "We'll see."

Claire gave no indication that she had overheard him. But she had.

And something very deep inside her warmed to his words.

Don't miss
DO YOU TAKE THIS MAVERICK?
by Marie Ferrarella, available August 2015 wherever
Harlequin® Special Edition books and ebooks are sold.

www.Harlequin.com

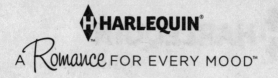

JUST CAN'T GET ENOUGH?

Join our social communities
and talk to us online.

You will have access to the latest
news on upcoming titles and special
promotions, but most importantly,
you can talk to other fans about your
favorite Harlequin reads.

Harlequin.com/Community

f Facebook.com/HarlequinBooks

▼ Twitter.com/HarlequinBooks

𝓟 Pinterest.com/HarlequinBooks

HARLEQUIN®

A Romance FOR EVERY MOOD™

**Stay up-to-date on all your
romance-reading news with the
Harlequin Shopping Guide,
featuring bestselling authors, exciting new
miniseries, books to watch and more!**

The newest issue will be delivered right to you
with our compliments! There are 4 each year.

Signing up is easy.

EMAIL

ShoppingGuide@Harlequin.ca

WRITE TO US

HARLEQUIN BOOKS
Attention: Customer Service Department
P.O. Box 9057, Buffalo, NY 14269-9057

OR PHONE

1-800-873-8635 in the United States
1-888-343-9777 in Canada

Please allow 4-6 weeks for delivery of the first issue by mail.

HSGSIGNUP

THE WORLD IS BETTER WITH

Romance

0880

Harlequin has everything from contemporary, passionate and heartwarming to suspenseful and inspirational stories.

Whatever your mood, we have a romance just for you!

Connect with us to find your next great read, special offers and more.